KISS OR KILL

Also by John Burton Thompson

One More For the Road

KISS OR KILL

JOHN B. THOMPSON

CUTTING EDGE

ISBN-13: 978-1-7344295-8-9

Published by
Cutting Edge Publishing LLC
PO Box 8212
Calabasas, CA 91372

CHAPTER ONE

"Some eagle," Matt Palmer, my lawyer friend once said, "snuck into that catbird's nest and laid an egg. You hatched out of it." Matt's the sort of friend who'll hand you a compliment just because he thinks you deserve it.

I accepted it the way I accept Matt's compliments because he always gave me the impression that he'd knock my teeth in if I didn't. If you gather from that remark that Matt's a rather overpowering individual, you'll be exactly right.

My father married a woman with a family already started. She had three boys. Later I came but for some reason I was a long time figuring out, she always seemed to resent me. It's true that her boys weren't much to look at and Matt tells me that I used to be pretty, but that seems a thin excuse for her to take out on me all the gall and sourness she could accumulate and that was plenty. Another thing, when Dad died, he left me half of everything he owned. To Mother, Jacob, Benjamin and Charles he left the other half, and although my father died loaded and their half was plenty they never got over me ... just one person and to them beneath contempt, getting half all to myself. That could have been a sore spot. Mother resented me all right but I don't think she hated me. The boys hated me with a hate this is really hard to understand ... not their reasons which I suppose were reasons enough, but the extent. I never knew anyone who could hate with such wholehearted zeal as those three boys.

Oh ... I'm John Abel McKnight. Dad in a burst of parental affection which I always thought he regretted, adopted Mother's three boys and we were the four McKnight boys of Galesburgh, Tennessee, a small town not too far from the Mississippi line.

Naturally, being younger, I was the butt of every cruel joke they could devise. To Mother they were just boyish pranks which she laughed off. They burned my feet with matches, put salt in my bed, accidentally pushed me off high places ... never high enough to hurt too much because I had learned the hard way and I never gave them a chance after I learned.

By the time I was fourteen, I began to give promise of being a cut above the rest physically. I was five eight then and weighed a hundred and sixty pounds. I had dark straight hair which I was proud of and kept glistening in place with whatever goo I could find. I guess, like Matt said, I was pretty. Jake, Benjy and Charley weren't pretty by any measurement. They were short and thick of body, with pale blonde hair and pale blonde eyes. My eyes were dark and my skin would take a tan the first day out in the sun. Theirs never would. I was getting tall and rangy, they being already grown would never make it. I was taller than any of them. They had whipped me with such frequency that I was afraid of them, but now I noticed that they began to sort of walk a half circle around me and inside I began to get bolder. One day I'd take them on and I'd whale them until they begged on their knees. I'd made up my mind to that way back when I was six.

They had all graduated from the University and were up to their eyes running Dad's far flung trucking empire, but they were never too busy to trip me up in anything I wanted to do very badly or to push me around. Matt Palmer once said if it was true about a child's psyche getting traumatized by ill treatment, mine would have been one great scar.

On the surface it would seem that I had no one to run to, but it wasn't that way at all and maybe that's why I didn't get too badly traumatized. Dad's lawyer, Matt Palmer, had always liked me and I hung around his place a great deal. Then at the age of fifteen there was Helga Ehrenberg. Helga, as Mother used to say in her grand way when trying to impress someone, was our "chamber maid." I never liked that term because to me a chamber was not a bedroom and I was mightily fond of Helga ... and she of me. She used to threaten to quit because of the way I was being treated but she didn't until I left home because I always talked her out of it. I thought I did anyhow.

Just how she ever wandered away from her father's farm in Iowa and drifted down to Tennessee, I never knew, but she did and Iowa lost one of its finest hunks of womanhood. Helga was really something. She was a big girl, about twenty-two, tall, husky, richly and smoothly hipped, her legs powerful and straight, her waist slim and her stomach flat, her chest was the most magnificent I had ever seen. Helga had a way about her, too, as the older boys found out when they tried her. She put a shiner on Benjy that lasted ten days and told off Jacob right in front of Mother which made him want to curl up and die. Charles got the hint and never tried. Helga wasn't overly moral, she was just choosy. She was affectionate to me and I ate it up and before she'd been there a year it became pretty plain that this affection would climb right on up the ladder to the rooftop.

She'd hug me tight when no one was looking and squeeze my face into one of her firm proudly lifted breasts that had never needed support. "You're my boy," she'd whisper and peck me a swift kiss on the lips. It always left me with a heavy storm going on inside but I never said anything mainly because I didn't know anything to say. Matt says I'm not dim witted, it just takes me longer to harvest the crop than a lot of people who are quick with the quip.

One late afternoon I was stirring up a lot of dust getting ready to attend a football game in Dayton, a small town ten miles way, when Jake came in and scotched the whole deal. I confronted Mother with it and I might not have been as diplomatic as I could have been but I was that sore.

"I want to know why I can't go to the Dayton game," I said shaking with rage. "I've been a lot farther than that to games and no one ever said anything."

"Maybe things should have been said before now," she replied sitting as was her way, stiffly in her chair, as prim as Queen Victoria and not nearly as good looking. She had wrinkled badly and always managed to blame it on me. She had been too old to have children, she liked to say, although she pretended to be at least ten years younger than she was. Having me had taken her beauty ... such as it was and she never forgave me for it.

"Jacob says all sorts of things go on at those games," she continued, her mouth screwed up in a knot of disapproval.

"Juvenile delinquency is rampant and you could very easily be led into all sorts of sin. You're very easily led you know, Abel." She never used John which was my father's first name or Jack which everyone called me. She was addicted to Biblical names.

"Seems to me like every game Jake, Benjy, and Chaz ever wanted to go to they went."

Her thin starved face flushed and tightened. "My sons ..." She disincluded me somehow. "My sons were always too level headed to get into trouble as you well know." She stood up and pointed an imperious finger. "You will go to your room and remain there until dinner is served."

I went, so mad I could hardly see where I was going. My eyes were flooded and I felt like I was choking to death. Not enough that they wouldn't let me play football, they were determined not to even let me watch if they could find an excuse.

I flung myself across the bed, clutching the bedspread and shuddering, trying to still the waves of exquisite fury that swept me. The moment I threatened to succeed, I'd whip it up again. I sobbed and clenched my teeth until my jaws ached. Then Helga walked in. I've often wondered about that day ... wondered if it could have happened unless everything had been in just the right spot at the right time. Jake' forbidding me to attend the game, my bout with Mother, my rage, Helga coming in to comfort me.

"What's the trouble, Jackie?" she said softly as she sat on the bed.

I tried to bury my head because I was ashamed of crying. "Get out," I yelled then yelled again for a different reason. Helga had swatted me on the behind with a big hand and it felt like she'd set fire to my pants.

"Snap at me like that again and I'll slap you silly," she said calmly. "I asked what the trouble was—or is."

I sat up, dried my eyes with my handkerchief and tried to tell her without crying again. I didn't make it but by the time I'd sobbed out the finish she had me cuddled close and was stroking my head, her own eyes wet with tears.

"One of these days," she said grittily, "I'm going to murder your miserable brothers and maybe include your mother. If it wasn't for you, I'd have been long gone and that's for sure."

I don't think I'd ever appreciated her more than now and something else was being born and it was strange and exciting. She released me and lay back on the bed, her breasts straining at the uniform front, the neck being open about one button too much, and I could see the thick rich bases and the creamy foothills. I felt antsy all over and all of a sudden I wanted to kiss her so I leaned forward and slid into the embrace of her left arm. She stroked my face and the back of my neck and hugged me close again. The pressure of her breasts on my chest made my ears ring and my head reel. They were warm and gentle to the touch. I became aware that I was being betrayed in a very vulnerable spot but right then it didn't seem to matter. She clutched me with another hug of quick affection and this time we were so close from knees to chin that she became aware of the betrayal but she didn't back away.

She smiled mistily at me. "You're getting to be quite a man, Jackie," she whispered and gave me her warm moist mouth. This was no peck. Her lips were loose but alive and her clean breath began to drag harshly through her nostrils. I think I went a little crazy and right there I discovered what a wonderful thing a kiss can be. In my madness I played with her lips, I mouthed this wonderful piece of confectionary and was thrilled out of my mind when I realized that she was getting as much of a charge out of it as I was. She ran a gentle hand behind my neck and crushed my lips against hers and her jaws slackened and I had my first experience with a roaring heady sweetness that darted from between her teeth. I met it with mine and for a space of time the world just stood still, then a physical convulsion struck me and all but blinded me. I hugged her so tight that she loosed a tiny groan of pain but she didn't mind. Her body seemed feverish, her loins soft and inviting, her flesh firm and unbelievably smooth in its satiny covering.

I relaxed and hid my head in her shoulder to keep her from seeing the tears.

She stroked me and murmured. "Sort of flattened you, didn't it?"

I nodded, afraid to speak, and experienced a chill of fear that she knew what had happened. She did know.

"It's all right, Jackie. You're getting to be a man now."

"You're … you're not mad at me, Helga?"

She chuckled and kissed me with a wet twisting motion that started my ears ringing again. "What for? For being a human being? I'm beginning to wonder if there are any human beings around here but you."

I kissed her again and again, the shattering wonder of her generous mouth shook me sorely. This time I did something I'd been wanting to do ever since she had come to the house. I placed a trembly hand gingerly on the summit of her right breast. She jumped as though stung and I jerked my hand away, mumbling an apology.

She laughed, took my hand and replaced it, holding it tight against the throbbing protuberance. "I'm not sore, Jackie," she whispered. "It just startled me, that's all."

Again our lips met. She seemed restless and I detected a strange wonderful motion on her part that I wanted to join and did. Suddenly she sat up and shook a long strong forefinger at me.

"Young man...and I do mean man, you're obstreperous, which is to say, bold, and you need your fanny tanned for the good of your soul."

I could see she wasn't sore so I grinned at her. "Now you sound like Mother."

"Oh Lord...I take it back then. I don't want to sound like her." Her face grew sober and her deep blue eyes seemed to engulf me. "Stand up here, Jackie."

She slipped from the bed and I stood up facing her. Her eyes were exactly on a level with mine.

"You've got some growing up to do and I'm the one to sit at the wheel." She put her arms around me, her eyes still serious. "Jackie, do you think you can keep what goes on between us to yourself?"

The question startled me. "Jeepers," I squeaked, hating it, "who'd I tell?"

"Don't tell anyone. I think you know I like you a great deal, don't you?"

"Oh ..." I shook my head and felt my eyes getting wet and that old stifling sensation attack my throat. "Helga, you've been the greatest...the very, very greatest. If you left...I couldn't stand the thought and held her close, feeling the outline of her magnificent body throb and quiver under my touch.

She caught my face in cool damp hands. "When you take your bath tonight, come to my room. They never come upstairs."

I couldn't speak. I just nodded my head and she was gone. I sank back to the bed and fought a battle with a foe I couldn't see...confusion. Did Helga mean what I thought she meant? How could she possibly? I inherited a streak of democracy from my father and for my money Helga was great people. All the term "chamber maid" did to me was make me sore. Not for an instant did I think of her as a lesser person.

The other three had their full store of snobbishness but none of it rubbed off on me. Perverseness might even help to explain my own tolerance. Anything they were, I was not going to be if I could help it.

Then, too, Helga wasn't the sort of a person you looked down your nose at. To begin with, it was a physical impossibility to anyone but a very tall man. Mother tried it a few times but Helga ignored her with such vacuumed indifference that Mother gave up. Mother was no match for her verbally, discovered it early and discretely never entered the lists with her again. Helga was a menial and unworthy of notice to the boys after she sat them down so hard and that was fine with her. Like I say, Helga was choosy. I like to think upon the fact that she had chosen me in preference to them in spite of my tender years.

What else could she want me to come to her room for? I wasn't afraid of discovery because more often than not I wasn't in my room anyway, having a certain facility for climbing out of my window, leaping out, catching a limb of the big live oak and doing a Tarzan to the ground. I could even get back in that way. No one in the house would enter Helga's room without knocking. I could either hide under her big old fashioned bed with its curtains, or in her closet. I wasn't worried about anyone coming in and searching her place. No one had the nerve.

I was so emotionally upset that I thought I'd be ill, then I hit upon a scheme I used a great many times afterward. I'd assume the best and at least be happy until I found out different.

CHAPTER TWO

I was still thinking ponderously when the tinkle of the dinner bell aroused me from the trance. With a bound I cleared the doorway and raced down the hall, took to the bannister rail and slid down it like an acrobat.

Benjy was at the landing to disapprove. "How many times have I told you not to do that?" he said severely. Benjy is the youngest of the three so I could remember some of his own youthful didoes.

"First person I ever saw do that was you," I reminded him. He flushed and bit his lower lip with vexation. "In that case," he said sourly, "I was as stupid as you are. It's a terrible thought but I must have been. In the light of mature wisdom, I say it's dangerous and if I see you do it again, I'll tear the tail off you!"

I looked at him squarely. He was the smallest of the three, too, and I'd mentally picked him as the first one I'd take on. "What'll you do, Benjy, in say ... oh, a couple of years when you won't be able to tear the tail off me?"

He flushed again. "Maybe I'd just better get on with it right now," he said sharply and stripped his belt from his trousers.

I reached into a corner where Chaz's golf clubs stood and pulled out a putter. "Just try it and if I don't spatter your brains all over the place, it won't be for the lack of trying."

"You'd look pretty silly, too," said Helga pointedly walking up and stopping within easy reach of Benjy.

He stuttered for a moment, choked with fury, then turning walked toward the west wing where he and the other boys had rooms.

"When I said you were getting to be a man, I wasn't kidding," she said and slipping her arm around my neck she gave me a quick hug. As she turned to go, I whispered, "See you later."

She winked and nodded and continued on her way.

As we sat down to dinner, Mother twisted her mouth, causing it to pucker like the closure of a sack. "I'm gratified, Abel, to see that you recovered from your pet of this afternoon. I'm glad you could see the possible evil of attending a game so far from town."

I didn't say anything because I was startled to realize that I had completely forgotten the game.

Benjy hadn't done any forgetting. "Just the same, he needs taking down a peg or two. He threatened to brain me a while ago with Charles' putter."

Jake thinned his already thin lips. "We'll see you at my room after supper," he said without heat. "If you bring a putter with you, you'll regret it."

I looked at them singly and individually. "'We'll see you.' So it's 'we' now." I laughed in their faces. Right at the moment a whipping didn't seem to amount to much. "Big tough guys. 'We'—" I felt my head getting hot. "Better make it good now, boys, because time's dwindling. It won't be long before I can take all three of you at once."

"You will leave the table at once," said Mother in an arctic voice. "At once. You will go to your room and remain there."

Jake looked up. "Not at the moment. Just take that chair in the corner. You have a date with us in my room immediately after dinner. I got up and sat grinning. Whippings never had the desired effect on me because long ago it had ceased being chastisement and developed into the three of them versus me…competition as it were. In five years they hadn't been able to wring a sound from me and I knew it irked the very hell out of them. Helga's touch always made my throat ache and it didn't take much from her to set my eyes to swimming, but the boys couldn't make me shed a tear no matter how hard they laid it on. After all, it was only physical pain. They weren't very imaginative and their favorite weapon was Dad's old razor strap. I think they must have read it somewhere. It hurt but not unbearably so and their methods never varied.

They marched me to the west wing and into Jake's room and shut the door. I could tell that a new deal was in the making in attitude if nothing else. I actually believe they were afraid of me. All the way from the dining room they looked as though they expected me to pull a gun and start blasting. As we passed the hall corridor where the stairwell is located, I caught a glimpse of Helga and she shook her hands over her head like a prize fighter and I grinned at her. I was actually enjoying the thing now. They were ashamed to tackle me together and afraid not to.

I stood in the middle of the room and looked at them still grinning. "Well, who's first to grab the snake. The other two will only get back pieces. That I promise." Tonight there wasn't going to be a mere whipping but a full scale battle. I already had my mind made up to one thing. I was going to wreck that room just like a tornado or like John Wayne in a movie bar room brawl.

Jake's room was full of very expensive furniture but the stuff looked spindly and frail as straw to me. It'd get a test tonight. I picked up a footstool. It was some sort of wicker stuff and as a weapon it wasn't much, but I had another use for it if Chaz would just make the first move. I nudged him a little.

"You've been doing a lot of looking but not much talking, Chazzy. What's the matter with you? That yellow streak finally showing?"

He advanced, white with rage. "Put that stool down," he said harshly and I'm sure he hoped, forcefully.

"Gladly," I said and threw it with all my might at his head. Naturally he ducked and the stool smashed squarely into the middle of Jake's long expensive beveled edge mirror on the wall and the sound it made was most gratifying. Jake let loose a scream of rage and lunged for me and I caught him coming in with a well-aimed foot and I felt the soft squish of his genitals as my foot crashed home.

He screamed and nosedived to the floor and I went off balance on purpose and upset a huge table with books, papers and two lamps on it. It all went down with a thunderous crash. Then Chaz got me around the neck and Benjy tried to grab my feet but I was moving too fast for that. Chaz and I reeled around the room careening wildly and finally I got a mouthful of his belly and tried to eat a hole in him. He bawled and let me go like I was hot. I reeled into the dresser and managed to send it flat with one lunge with all I had behind it. Benjy then got me around the legs and tripped me and Chaz sat on me. Since they outweighed me an average of fifty pounds apiece, that ended the first installment. Jake was still moaning and scrabbling around on the floor like a beheaded fowl.

"I'll go help him," said Chaz, starting to get off my back.

"The hell you will," screamed Benjy. "That'll just leave me."

"Sure," I yelled, getting into the spirit of things. "Don't you dare leave Benjy here with this maneater."

"Shut up," snarled Chaz and picking up a chair leg that had been knocked loose clouted me in the head with it and I lost interest in the proceedings.

That was a great day in my life for a lot of reasons. Another one became obvious just as I was waking up from Chaz's blow to the head with the chair leg. Chaz and Benjy still had me down but we'd raised such a noisy brand of hell what with my wrecking operations and a lot of screaming and yelling, that Mother had come in to see what it was all about.

"What on earth are you trying to do?" she hissed, just as I came back to the living. I lay still hoping to hear how she felt about this business of trying to knock my brains out.

"You'll alarm the servants, the neighbors and what would you say if that old fool of a constable Winters would hear and come poking his nose in here?" She didn't know it but a great deal more potent personality was even then on his way. Helga who had seen everything from the back gallery window to Jake's room had made a phone call.

"He just went berserk," snarled Chaz. "I had to clout him with a chair leg to quiet him down."

"And what if you've killed him? With the motive you have, you'd have a very pretty time explaining that to a jury."

"Good God Almighty," bleated Benjy going instantly into a purple funk. He caught my hair which I wore long and began to jerk my head around and slap my face. "Oh—God—God, please don't let him be dead."

Jake, who'd just recovered enough to sit up, was watching, his eyes burning with hate and glazed with agony. "Shut up, you braying jackass," groaned Jake. "Shut up—I've got to get to a hospital. That son of a bitch has just about done for me."

Mother, whose only concern up till now was what they'd tell a jury if they'd killed me, hauled off and lost her ladyhood when Jake called me that name.

"If I was a man, I'd kick you again," she blazed.

Jake must have thought that his whole world had come apart. He hadn't meant any reflection on Mother.

She turned to Benjy and Chaz. "Get off the boy."

They got up and I came slowly to my feet with a great deal of melodramatic groaning and effecting to still be half out of my mind. I looked like I'd been brained—and I was making all the capital of it I could.

Right at that moment Matt Palmer, whom Helga had called, walked in and stood framed by the doorway nearly filling it. Matt is six four and weighs about two hundred and forty pounds. His face is craggy and handsome in an ugly sort of way, his head is leonine and covered with tumbling masses of stiffly curled black hair. His shoulders are not quite as broad as a billiard table. In all about as overpowering sort of a guy as I ever met in my life.

"Where," he asked, his voice laced with acid, "is the monster?"

"What monster?" squeaked Benjy, pitiably relieved to discover that I wasn't dead—for his own good reasons, of course.

"Well, from the looks of this room, Jake weeping on the floor holding his, er...holding himself, Jack's head split open and his face covered with gore, must have been a monster and a real rough one, too."

I was so relieved to see him that I sat weakly on Jake's bed noticing as I did that I was dripping a goodly amount of claret over his snowy bedspread.

"You're an ass," Chaz said with a snarl. "We were forced to administer a whipping to your precious Jack there, and he fought back."

"It has been reliably reported that certain species of rats will fight back when pushed far enough. What did you bust him with, a lead pipe?"

"A chair leg," shouted Chaz turning red, "and not very hard either."

"Is that tomato catsup he's leaking all over?"

"I—well, the chair leg cut his scalp a bit."

"Why are you here, Mr. Palmer?" said Mother frigidly. "I don't recall sending for you."

"I heard from a little bird that there was a riot going on here so I thought I might help." He threw his big head back and roared with laughter. "A sixteen year old boy gets his dander up and takes on three grown men. Boy, this is rich." Then very suddenly, as it his way on occasions, he went from laughing to a searing scowl in a split second. He turned to Mother. "Just how much of this do you allow around here and don't get imperious with me. I'm still chairman of the McKnight trust and as such I needn't remind you that I can deal you more misery than you can stuff in your knitting bag."

"It is not, to my knowledge, against the law for an elder brother to chastise a younger with his mother's approval."

The jovian scowl deepened. "I'm going to take the boy to the clinic to get his head sewed up. I'm going to ask Dr. Wheeler if in his opinion this sort of treatment can be glossed over under the heading of chastisement. In fact, I think the district attorney should know and certainly Judge Bernstein who was a great friend of your late husband's."

Mother went pipe clay pale and caught the back of a chair that was still in one piece. "Please, Mr. Palmer, this whole thing has been a most unfortunate happening. My sons were merely protecting themselves."

"I wonder if you know how silly that sounds. One boy, three grown men nearly twice his size."

Jake vomited on the floor and made quite a smelly mess.

Mother knelt beside him and made soothing sounds and dabbed at his wet forehead with a wispy handkerchief. She looked up at Matt. "Please call an ambulance. My son is in danger. He may be mortally injured."

Matt looked at her as he would a stray cat. "This other son ... I mean this orphan on the bed is bleeding all over the place. My concern is with him. If Charley and Benjy and you can't get Jake to the hospital, then I'm afraid I couldn't either." He looked at me like he wanted to break my arm. "Get the hell off that bed and come with me.

I grinned and did as he said.

Well ... they sewed up my head but they had to shave a spot of hair that hurt more than the needle did. After the stitching job, Matt took me to his house.

Matt's wife Bertha ... he calls her Bert and I call her Mamma, and Ginger made me feel like I was pretty important the way they bustled around. Ginger wore a quilted housecoat of flowered satin, primly buttoned and sashed, and the way it slipped over her smooth skin made my mouth water. I know she didn't have a thing on under it ... but I was a part of the scenery around Matt's and no one gave it a thought but me. For a spell, I couldn't think of anything else.

"These clothes are ruined," said Mamma positively. "Take them off."

"Right here?" I squeaked on that one and it sent Ginger into stitches.

Mamma laughed. "No. In Jerry's room. Jerry was their son who was attending the University. He was first string end on the freshman football team and a real great guy.

I bathed, dressed and went back down and Mamma asked, "Did you have dinner, Jackie?"

"No ma'am. Mother made me leave the table before I'd started eating."

Matt gave a rumble and knocked his pipe out in the fireplace. He took a chair. "All right. You're sewed up and presentable. Now what's with this business over there tonight?"

I grinned at Matt. "That's right, I was trying to think where I should start."

"The beginning has been said to be a good place."

I shook my head. "What happened tonight had its beginning so far back I can't even remember it. Better I should start with today, maybe." I took a deep breath. "I've been going to football games wherever they're played. I expected to follow the team out of town tonight and was getting ready when Jake came in and said I couldn't go. I went to Mother and as usual she took his side. Juveniles are all winding up in jail and going to the dogs according to her and it's Jake's belief that no good happens at football games.

"What the hell does she consider you?" he growled, "a spider monkey that escaped from a zoo?"

"Oh dear ..." Mamma was outraged.

"She said that and sent me to my room to stay till dinner. On my way to dinner, I slid down the bannisters and Benjy took his belt off to whip me. I took a club out of Chaz's bag and threatened to brain him with it. I thought I'd gotten away with it until he told Jake about it at dinner. That got me sent from the table with no dinner and that's what the ruckus was about."

"Tell me," said Matt, "How did you happen to pick tonight as D-day?"

I said, "Oh … it'd been boiling a long time. Tonight I just got my fill. I wasn't sitting still for a beating anymore."

Matt thoughtfully filled his pipe. He looked at Mamma. "So when a boy decides to be a man and not a dog to cuff around, he gets his head split open."

Mamma's full lovely mouth thinned and tightened. "Maybe I'd better not say anything. I might say too much."

"It's pretty hard to know what to say," said Matt with a ferocious scowl. "Everyone knows Jack's a damn pain in the neck and has a greater store of snide annoyances than any hundred kids in town. Devilment comes naturally to him. I suppose he makes Jake, Benjy and Charlie feel impotent or something."

"Why," I asked, "do they hate me?"

He glanced at me quickly, then his eyes fell. "I don't know and what I think doesn't matter."

"What you think," I told him with a rare streak of his own frankness, "means more to me than anyone I know."

Matt blushed and Ginger giggled. He took it out on her. "One more giggle out of you and I'll broil your butt right here in front of Jack."

"What would happen to my half if I was to die?" I asked.

He looked at me sharply. "Boy, you're full of questions tonight. What on earth ever made you think of that?"

"Well, Mother said when she thought I was unconscious, that if I was dead they'd have a happy time convincing a jury that it was all a bit of chastisement, as she likes to call it."

Matt smacked his big hands together. "So you've been toying around with what the motive is. Well, since you've already thought of it, your half reverts to the estate in the event of your demise."

"My God," said Mamma turning white, "what a thing to have to live with."

I shrugged. "Mother's against it because of how it will look. The other three wouldn't have the nerve. What started the fire was when I threw a stool at Chaz, broke the mirror and then kicked Jake in the … kicked him."

"Kicked him where?" Ginger wanted to know.

"None of your business," snapped Matt. "That room … it looked like a cyclone had passed through."

I grinned. "That was something I'd made my mind up to before we ever got into the room. I had a ball. It was worth this head even."

CHAPTER THREE

Mamma let it go at that but it was plain she didn't like it. Matt's car was under the carport way in the back of the big house. When we were just about to go out of the darkened vestibule onto the carport, he muttered something ugly. "Dammit, I forgot my keys." He turned and went back into the house proper.

Ginger, who had come along, came up to me and whispered, "I'm really sorry about everything, Jack, and I didn't mean anything giggling at you."

I laughed. "I know that. It just hit me at a bad time."

Then she came into my arms, fully intending to catch one of our quick giggly kisses but that was one time she was fooled. I'd learned how. Her lips were satin soft and as usual she tried to dart away to go into her giggling session but I'd slipped an arm about her neck and held her tight. She started, her lips stiffened and her body grew taut, then as I wove my spell with my newly learned technique she gradually went lax and her mouth went soft. When her jaws slackened, I drove hard for more freedom and her mouth opened for something for which she was not prepared. When our tongues met a deep gusty sound come from deep in her chest. She went limp in my arms and hearing Matt's footsteps, I released her and she staggered a little, a hand going to her mouth.

"Ooooo … Jack …"

"All ready?" Matt said.

"Yes sir." I was glad it was dark in the vestibule because he'd have noticed Ginger's attitude instantly. She was leaning back against the wall, her eyes starry and wide, her lips parted and a look of wondrous stupefaction on her face. I could see her because my eyes were adjusted to the light. I followed Matt out and when I was ready to go through the door, she touched my arm.

"Come back soon, Jack," she whispered.

I nodded and went to the car.

As I sat down beside Matt, he whacked me solidly across the belly. He's that way. Sometimes he'll nearly knock you down but it's merely his way of showing affection. He grinned at me.

"How was that for getting you off the hook?" He backed the car out of the driveway and into the street.

"Er ... sir?"

"All right, play dumb. Boy, you didn't just want to go home, you were in a fever to go home, Now why?"

I went cold all over. This was something Matt and I had never discussed although he had made it very plain to me that I was to come to him at any time, no matter what the problem was. I was silent so long, he said, "If it's a secret, son, it's okay. I was just curious."

I shook my head and thought a while longer. "Matt, you and I never talked on this subject before. I don't know exactly how to tell you."

"Maybe this'll be a help. You've never seen, heard or imagined anything that I haven't done and imagined ten times over. I have a suspicion it has to do with a girl. Since there is only one girl at your house that'd bear a second look, it must be Helga who is a delight to the eye any way you take her. She was the one who called me. She sounded very concerned."

I shrugged. "I guess I knew I couldn't keep anything from you."

"When did it happen?"

"Today ... that is, nothing's happened ... Matt ..." I looked at him hard. "She wouldn't like it one bit if I told anyone."

"Do I impress you as a man who runs around blabbing to every ass who'd listen something I know is a very private and probably very precious secret?"

"No sir."

"All right then. I'm not just idly curious, Jack. I have a reason for wanting to know."

Then I told him. Everything there was to tell and I got tremendous relief from the telling.

He nodded when I finished. "It's something every boy is going to learn. You're luckier than most. She's probably no fool."

"She's not," I agreed stoutly. "She's smart as a whip. I wonder why she holds a job like she's got. She could do better."

"It's like teaching. Most of them are underpaid but they teach anyway." He whacked me again. "Can't say as I blame you for being in a fever to get home. I've seen her, boy, and she's something."

I mopped the sweat from my face with a hand that jerked like a wino's.

Matt's big chuckle grated again. "That was sort of hard for you to get out, wasn't it?"

"It sure was. Like I say, though, I can't keep anything from you doesn't seem like."

"That's all to the good. If you're wrong, I'll tear you to shreds about it. If you're confused, we'll talk it out. If you're scared, we'll belly up to it and see if it deserves to be scared of. I can't see anything gained by nursing a lot of things in your sixteen year old mind that run around in circles looking for a place to go."

I gave a short laugh. "Most things in my sixteen year old mind run in circles. About the only time I can sort 'em out is when I talk to someone ... you or Helga."

"What do you think of Ginger?"

"Oh ... man ... She's strictly at the summit, high out and far gone." He'd surprised me again and I'd spewed out with it like a cheap Roman candle.

"Look, Jack," he said, his voice a soothing rumble. "I'm not going to jump down your throat. I just want us to have a straight talk about Ginger."

"But gosh, Matt ... Ginger and I ... well, we never ..."

"I'm not saying you did. Now answer me something. Did you ever think of it?"

I shook my head and dropped my eyes. "I guess ... I have."

He touched my shoulder and it was as gentle as a feather. "Of course you have. You're human, aren't you?"

I looked up aghast at his understanding. I couldn't say anything. I just looked at him.

He smiled faintly. "Find that strange, do you? I suppose so. Son, let me tell you something. It hasn't been too many years ago that I was sixteen years old.

"Matt, what do you want me to say? That I'll stop coming around? Maybe that'd be the best idea because believe me, Ginger is a grass fire ready to burn something up."

He laughed. "I'm a father but I can see the signs, too. That's why I wanted to talk to you before anything happened. Suppose we'd been gone to a party or a show? Tell me honestly, Jack, what would have happened?"

I looked at my feet and wished I could die. I just knew he hadn't seen that kiss.

"I'm not trying to embarrass you and I'm not jumping on you.

A thought caught me and it burst out. "What about other fellows, Matt?"

He nodded. "That's a good question. We watch her pretty close with everyone but you. We don't allow any late single dating. Parties, shows, dances, things like that but no boy girl moonlight hole in the woods sort of things."

"Why don't you watch me?" I asked, wondering when I could stop being a fool and start making sense if I was going to talk.

He put his hand on my shoulder again. "Because I don't want to. I don't want to have to. If it's news to you that around our house you're pretty special people, then you're a fool.

"What do you want me to do?"

Matt went into one of my silences, maybe longer. I can't say what she'll do. Neither am I an ass who jabbers that his daughter won't do any such thing. Hell, I don't have the faintest notion what my daughter will do. I simply don't want trouble as I said before."

"Did you ever have trouble?"

He straightened a little. "No, I didn't."

"Why?"

"Because my Dad knew people. He knew his son. He got me aside one day and explained to me in plain language that when a girl gives herself to a man, she's given him every damn possession she has worth anything. When he accepts it, he is suddenly loaded with responsibilities ... Follow me, boy?"

"Yes sir."

"All right. He owes her physical protection and he owes her a closed mouth. Men for some peculiar reason are notorious braggarts and many a girl's reputation has been laid waste by a loose mouth. I don't want any of this to happen to Ginger. I don't want it to happen to you. If you and she ever get to the altar, I want you to have gotten there the right way after you're both mature enough to tell one shoe from the other."

I thought it, I had to say it. "And in the meantime?"

He looked sadly out of the car window. "I don't know. One damn thing sure. I'm not going to spy on the two of you. You're both very close to me. I'm not telling you what not to do because it wouldn't do any good." He glared at me. "What do you know about this man-woman stuff?"

"Not much, I'm afraid."

"Have you ever taken a woman ..."

"No ... no ... no." I was in a frenzy to get him stopped. I was panting and sweating again.

"All right. Here are a few things you should know." And he unloaded on me. In plain understandable English he laid it on the line and I gobbled up every word. His attitude impressed me then. Think how it impressed me years later when I'd think back and wonder what would have happened to me if it hadn't been for Matt Palmer.

"It can lay waste to a life. It can corrode your guts and morals until they are nothing but shreds and I'm not talking about blue-nose morals. I'm talking about pride, intellectual morality, the opinion you have of yourself. The ability to tell a man from a son of a bitch. The possession of enough humanity to know that your own freedom is like the wind in the trees until it runs head on with another's freedom." He twisted around and pinned me with hard brown eyes. "You've got a streak of honesty in you that came straight from your dad. You tell yourself you can't tell me a lie but that's not the whole story. I'm telling you I don't want my daughter to be a mother before she's through being a child."

"Have you talked to Ginger?"

"Not like this. Ginger's not as deep as you and I let her mother run that side of things. I don't think I could talk like this to her unless she came to me with a question. Bert can answer any question Ginger's likely to ask. I've talked to Jerry. Bert and I divide the chore."

I pondered a moment. "Yes, but will Mamma answer it like you would one of mine?"

He sighed. "Probably not. Son, there's the male and there's the female. If a man thinks like a woman, then he's not much of a man. If a woman thinks like a man, she's for the birds. Maybe someday male and female will get together on a common ground on equal terms." He grinned. "But a lot of fun will be lost, I imagine. Now let me take you home.

"Gee, Matt, I'm sure glad you did and I can tell you one thing. I wouldn't harm a hair of Ginger's head for all the tea in China."

"Don't go making me any gilded promises," he snapped, "then feel like a twenty-four carat heel if you fail. Ginger's a load of attraction. She's young and as silly as they come."

I was a little shocked. "Matt, you can't mean Ginger's loose."

"Not the way you put it. You're around all the time. You'll have opportunity. The others won't until she's a lot older. Maybe by then she'll have some sense. Until then ... I'm telling you all this to guard against what might happen until then. Ruination doesn't come from the sex act, Jack, it comes from stupidity, carelessness, ignorance, callousness, the lack of regard for the woman, anything that will cause a man to duck his responsibilities. I'm not inviting you to take my daughter to bed. I'm trying to be as sensible as I can about it and prevent trouble for you, her and everyone concerned."

I didn't say anything else and he seemed satisfied. When he let me out he got out and said, "I'm coming in and talk to your mother. You beat it to bed." He caught a handful of my side and pinched me painfully. "And I said to bed ... understand?"

I grinned. "Sure straight to bed."

"Sure, straight to bed ... but whose?"

"A man's got to watch his ethics. No loose talk, remember?"

"Ah ... shut up."

I stood there looking at him in the dim light and a thickness rose in my throat. "Matt ... I want to thank you ..."

"Don't ever try to choke back like that around me," he said in a strangely quiet voice. "A man needs to cry every now and then for an outlet.

"Did you ever , , , cry after you ... were grown?"

"Who me? I drip like a bastard and I've had to beat the ass off a lot of fools who thought it was funny, too."

We went into the house and were met at the door by Mother. Jake, I assumed, was in the hospital and right then I didn't care what state he was in. Benjy and Chaz were either with him or out of sight.

"How is the boy?" asked Mother. She was curious, I suppose. She surely didn't seem overly concerned.

"His skull isn't fractured, if that's what you mean," said Matt shortly. "They took eight stitches."

Mother was pale and looked ill.

"I think," said Matt shortly, "that you and I had better have a little talk."

"As you wish," she replied, twisting her mouth. "In the library."

" 'Night, kid," he said and gave me an affectionate push.

" 'Night, Matt, and thanks for everything."

I managed to get the door to the library cracked before they got settled.

"I don't think, Mr. Palmer," she said as she arranged her dress primly over her knees, "that we have anything to discuss."

"I'm not surprised that you feel that way," he retorted. "Just the same we'll have the talk. Dr. Wheeler is a man of few words and when I asked if he'd remember this incident in case I ever needed him, he replied that his memory was excellent. I'm not one of these so-called moderns who think that moral persuasion is the answer to young rebels and their pranks. My son Jerry can recall without too much trouble when I marked him from his ankles to his shoulder blades with oak limbs. Not many times because done with justice and done right, it rarely takes more than a few good ones. I've watched this boy creep from your house like a skulking dog and come to mine for a little affection and on many occasions for a square meal."

"I do not need instruction on how I shall discipline my son and if he has been running to you every time he's corrected, then I shall put a stop to that, too."

"He hasn't been running to me every time he's been corrected because I've done a little investigation on my own and the servants state that it is rare that any of you speak to him except to criticize. He'd be over there all the time. However, if this is repeated, be very sure that I shall take legal action, the point of which will be to declare this house and you as his mother unfit for the rearing of a young son."

"Indeed," she said stiffly, "and what will you do with him? Place him in a foster home?"

"In a manner of speaking. I'll place him in my own home and I think the court will agree that it will be a good place for him."

"Then you'll be in a good position to get your claws on his money, won't you?" she screamed, turning purple and leaning forward, a vile, poisonous witch.

"It is my opinion," he said carefully, "and it shall be my story, should more come of it, that this incident tonight was exactly that. A crude attempt to murder the boy so that his half of the estate would revert to you and your sons."

Mother went white and sank back in her chair. "You couldn't believe that. You wouldn't do it."

"You must have believed it," he said bluntly. "That's the first thing you said when you got to Jake's room tonight. You thought the boy was still out. He wasn't. He heard every word you said. I heard the latter part of it myself."

Matt got up, gave her a scorching glance and said, "Think it over."

He walked out like Richard, Coeur de Lion, leaving Mother staring at the carpet lost in deep thought or shocked past moving.

CHAPTER FOUR

"Okay, eavesdropper," came a soft voice at my shoulder. "You can come to bed now."

I almost jumped out of my pants. It was Helga. She had on a robe of heavy slipper satin that might have been a little bigger for the best fit but on Helga it was devastating.

"How'd you know I was here?" I whispered as we moved out on the gallery.

"I snoop," she said calmly. You all right?"

"I'm fine," I said.

Her room was first from the back stairs and we stopped. She drew me close and stroked my head. "Take a bath ..."

"I had one at Matt's."

"Good. Go put your robe on and come back." She kissed me and I sort of reeled off to my room with my ears ringing crazily.

I undressed and sat on my bed in a kind of chill. This was H-hour for sure and I was scared to death. I clenched my teeth, slipped on a light maroon robe and without stopping to think ... if I had I might have chickened out, opened my door, closed it carefully and went to Helga's room. She met me at the door, laughed and pulled me inside closing and latching the portal.

"Jackie ... Jackie ..." She held my head close and stroked it. She liked to do that and I liked it, too. "Jackie, I'm not going to eat you." I guess I must have looked scared.

"I know." I quavered then I remembered how much better it was with Matt when I'd talk it out completely. I looked into her enormous blue eyes and sort of shivered. "Helga, I'm scared to death."

She laughed and kissed me. "I suppose you are, poor darling." I was conscious of the pressure of her breasts naked beneath the robe, the waterfall of shiny golden hair that she had taken down and was now floating about her face making her look like a Viking princess. "Come here and sit with me," she said. There was a really nice couch in her room and we sat on it. I was relieved because it seemed to defer any early decision.

From the first kiss that sent blood pounding in my ears, I sensed that something was different. At the time I thought it was me because I was in such an intense itch for the touch of her mouth and the ecstatic wonders of her big satin skinned body that I sort of pushed things rather than let her do it and the result sent her into crumpled boneless submission and I handled her at my will. I was doing famously, my new talent at kissing wrenching harsh exhalations from her and my hand had found her right breast and had been struck rigid with electric sensation which was no less than the upheaval of her body that tossed me as though I'd been a sack of hay. Yes, I was doing famously when all of a sudden it seemed that an avalanche of reaction struck me all at once. It was a build-up of the effects of the hours preceding the present, the blow on the head, the visit to the doctor, the visit to Matt's house, the kiss and stunned reaction of Ginger, and now something that I'd dreamed of right enough but had never dared think it'd happen. I slumped and rolled away from her, my face drenched with sweat and my heart about to pound me to pieces. She saw it instantly.

"Jackie ... what's the matter, darling ... What's the matter?"

I tried to straighten up but I was as weak as a cat and started crying again. Helga knew probably more then than I would when I was thirty and she sized the situation up quickly. "No wonder," she said, all business and objectivity. "You've been beaten ..." She was bustling around doing something. "Had your head cracked and enough without it to drive a kid crazy …" She thrust it in my hand and it was cold and damp. A glass of something. "Drink it," she commanded.

Between sobs I sipped at it and I thought it was going to sear me brown.

"Go ahead," she said. "It's whiskey with a little water and ice. It'll put you right in no time."

The stuff made my head whirl faster than it already was and I began to feel not there, like sitting on the roof of Madison Square Garden looking down on a fight.

"Now to bed," I heard her say and my teeth began to chatter like castanets. She made me swallow the rest of the drink and as I started for the bed and lifted a knee to get into it, she stripped the robe from me. I wasn't even there enough to be embarrassed but just slid between sheets as cold as iron. By the time she got in with me, I was shaking so hard that the warm touch of her magnificent body didn't mean a thing but I began to quiet down and soon drifted off to sleep.

It must have been past midnight when I waked. I don't think I ever felt so comfortable. I was rested, the chill had been replaced by a warmth that was so delightful it should have had a taste. Helga'd covered us well and we now faced each other. She was sleeping sweetly, her breath coming deep and regular. She had cuddled me to get me warm and her left arm was still a pillow. It was like I was in the center of a cocoon with her. All my senses seemed super sharp. I could smell the antiseptic the doctor had used on my head, the faint fragrance that came from Helga's hair that sprawled on her pillow like a fan of spun gold, the dim echoes of the soap she had used in her bath and from the opening in the cover that gaped between us came the rarest of all perfumes that you'll never be able to buy in a bottle. Helga was a fabulous incensory, healthy strong and the slight draft of warm air that came to my nostrils was loaded with woman. The odor of clean exultant womanhood. She was as clean as soap and water could make her, she was without a stitch of clothing. I seemed to draw strength from her, strength that she had in such quantity, and I so little. I eased closer to her, very careful not to awaken her, but I had forgotten something and by the time I had fitted her and was listening to the bells that rang in my ears from the stupefying exultation, my forgetting caused her to wake.

She opened her eyes and instantly they were warmly smiling and her lips followed suit. "Feeling better, Jackie?"

I was a little embarrassed now. "I feel fine."

"Good." She held me closer and I was now so acutely conscious of her that I was almost out of my mind.

She was a woman and I was a man. I could look down on her but she had to look up at me. A man ... I grew another foot then unraveled and came apart at the seams. Gone was the feeling of immense possession. Gone was the impression of being a giant. I had been struck down in midstride so to speak.

She relaxed with such sudden completeness that I thought she had fainted but finally she opened her eyes that were pearly with repleteness, soft with unspeakable affection. I tried to move but she clutched me and held me.

A man knows when he has been a man or has just simply one of a party of two. The rigors that would sweep her fabulous body, the light of adoration in her eyes, the gentle sweetness of her smile, a smile that was mine alone, a sort of semaphore between the two of us to denote possession. My stomach turned loose with a sputtering growl you could have heard thirty feet away.

"Go ahead and growl," I said, "you can't bite."

She laughed and held me tight for a moment, then started. "Jackie, did you eat dinner?"

"Well, no. Matt's wife was going to give me some, I'm sure, but I think she forgot. We all did."

Helga uttered a phrase or so in Swedish and I'm sure it wasn't nice. She slid from the bed, slipped into her robe with a deft grace that made my skin tingle.

"I'll be back in a flash with something to eat."

She came back soon with a bed tray and two huge roast beef sandwiches, a glass and a quart of milk. She arranged it with me still in bed, then drew up a chair close to the bed. "All right, fall to."

I did and cleaned it up in no time. She took the tray then handed me my robe. "Back to your room and brush your teeth. That's part of the training program. Nothing can excuse an unclean body. Your mouth is part of your body."

The things I'd learned today…Matt and Helga and I think every one of them registered. Matt had taught me the value of avoiding hurting a girl, physically and otherwise, especially a young girl, and I couldn't help think when he was talking that he was thinking about Ginger.

I brushed my teeth with care and went back to Helga's room, moving as I had learned by necessity with the stealth of a mouse.

She patted the bed and I sat beside her. "What happened to Jake?" I wanted to know.

"Dr. Gillein came to see him. They carted him off to the clinic. Seems that you broke a blood vessel or something where it could be seriously inconvenient for him. As I got it, they're going to open him up and tie off the bleeder."

"Open him up there?"

"Yes. He was swollen and purple as a grape down there."

"Where were you?"

"Snooping. I heard everything, saw just about everything."

"What did they tell the doctor?"

"They said it was an accident. He let it drop for the moment but I'll bet he got the dope as soon as they were out of hearing."

I couldn't stay away from her any longer so I kissed her and bent her back on the bed. "I love you, Helga," I said brokenly and had to hide my face to keep her from seeing the tears.

She sat up slowly and pulled me with her. "Jackie, I want to talk to you about that."

"About what?"

"Love. Love is a misused word. I left my home because I thought I was in love and I couldn't stand it when it turned out he didn't want anything but my body. I'm sure you're smart enough to know you're not the first. As a matter of fact, neither was he. It's so easy for love to get mixed up with something like this. I love you, too ... that is, I feel what you feel. A while ago there was no world but this room and no one but us."

"Then you think what I feel isn't love?"

"I didn't say that. What I mean is, any love that begins this young can't stand the beating it has to take. You're just a baby, Jackie ..." She hugged me tight. "A man, too, but a baby really. You've just broken the shell. You grew up like a sunflower today but you've so much more growing to do" She cocked her head at me. "What about Ginger?"

"What about her?" I'd been too quick with it. Too sharp.

She smiled and pressed her nose against mine. "It was a plain question and you bit at me. So you like Ginger?"

"I like her," I said defensively. "She's cute ... I think she sort of likes me"

I wasn't being honest with Helga and she knew it. She didn't say anything. Just looked at me.

"All right," I said miserably. "What do you want me to say?"

"Nothing, Jackie. I just want you to think."

"I've thought. Now what?"

"Haven't you felt pretty much for Ginger what you feel for me?"

I nodded. "I guess you're right and that makes me pretty silly, doesn't it?"

"Not at all. Just immature You're just sixteen.

"You can say that again. Helga, why is a girl like you working here like this?" That was something I'd been thinking about for a long time.

She was silent for a while, then she said, "I'm afraid you've blown me up all out of size, Jackie. Emotions do that to you. Right now you probably think I'm the most ..."

"The most and the best and the greatest the loveliest…" I choked on the rest and couldn't go any further. She hugged me. "Thank you, my knight in the shiningest armor. I'm glad that's the way I affect you.

"Get married," I said and cursed under my breath because if she did, I'd lose her.

She gave me our secret smile "I'll do that someday, Jackie, but I'll never forget my knight… Never."

She didn't and I didn't although people who say such things and mean them at the time rarely ever do anything about them. Not Helga and I. We never lost contact although we were pretty far apart sometimes.

Her mouth found mine and we lay back on the bed letting the singing fever seek and find us again. The night was ours, hers and mine, and no words could ever really tell what we made of it.

When I woke the next morning, she had on a pair of light tan panties of a knit so thin that the healthy pink of her skin shone through That and nothing else. She was seated at her dressing table brushing her heavy masses of golden hair until it crackled with life and shone like metal. I lay there for a moment so relaxed and comfortable it seemed a shame to move but I couldn't stand the sight of her very long. I slid off the bed and approached her from behind. She saw me in the mirror and smiled a welcome. She put down her brush but she didn't turn… just watched me in the mirror and smiled a welcome. She shivered and her fine skin pebbled from sensation. I hugged her close and buried my face in the dense jungle of her soft hair. My own skin tried to crawl off my bones.

"You," she said softly, "have to go to school."

"I know." I glanced at her clock. It was a quarter to seven. If I got ready by eight, I'd be on time. I reached for her lips and she turned her head to meet me. Just like last night they were so soft and eagerly responsive that my heart ached fiercely. "I don't have to go right now, do I?"

She disengaged my hands, stood and let me fit her like a glove, our lips hungrily alive and seeking. "Not right now," she answered when she could catch her breath.

Breakfast was not a pleasant meal. Benjy and Chez looked murder at me. Mother maintained a tight lipped silence. I didn't say anything either and though I was still riding my victory high I couldn't break a fear that had ridden me all my life.

"It does seem," said Mother at length, "that you could in decency ask about your brother since you were the one who assaulted him so brutally."

This I needed. "How is he?"

"The doctor had to operate. He was bleeding internally. You'll suffer for it, Abel. I make you the solemn promise."

"Did Jake ask about me?"

She gave me a peculiar look as much as to say, "Why should he?" "I don't recall that your name was mentioned."

"I did my bleeding externally," I said getting a little warm behind the neck. "As for your promise, Matt and I did considerable talking about that."

She gripped her coffee spoon as though she'd like to cut my throat with it. "Indeed. And at what conclusion did you arrive?"

"We decided there wasn't much you could do other than kill me and we doubted that you'd have the nerve since no matter how I met with an end, you four would be prime suspects due to the way the property will shift." I looked at Chaz and Benjy. Benjy was frightened but Chaz's face was stony cold with hate. I smiled at them. "In fact, after today when he talks with the judge and the D.A., you'd better take pretty good care of me. Accidents happen and Matt, I've heard said, can bend evidence like a pretzel."

I drank the last of my coffee and left them at the table, my step a lot jauntier than I felt.

Matt came to get Ginger then made her run me down.

"Dad wants to see you," she said looking so straight at me with her clear greenish hazel eyes that I felt naked.

"Yeah ... where?"

"Over by the gym."

I took one look at Matt and had a quick impulse to duck the meeting, knowing all along I didn't have the nerve. He didn't look sore but when Matt looks sore usually he isn't. He didn't look anything. He just looked at me like I was a dead fish on the wharf.

"Get in," he said metallically. "Ginger, get in the back and don't open your yap."

"Something wrong?" I asked squeaking dangerously on the last word. I could feel rather than hear Ginger giggle.

"Just wanted to ask you a few things. What've you been telling at home?"

"Nothing ..."

"Don't lie to me, Jack."

I squirmed. "Give me a minute, Matt, please."

He struck me on the leg hard enough to raise a frog and I knew everything was all right, almost.

Finally I said, "I got talked to and I talked back."

"That's bad," he said.

"What should I have done?"

He sighed like a mountain slide. "Hell, how do I know? Couldn't you have just stayed quiet like you do when I'm trying to get something out of you?"

"Maybe that would have been the best. How'd you know?"

"Benjy and Charlie went to Tom Morton's office about noon and had cats all over the office."

"About what?"

"Seems you convinced them that no matter what sort of accident happened to you, I could twist it and make it come out the electric chair for them."

"Well, Mother told me about Jake and made me some sort of solemn promise that I'd never get away with it. I didn't know what she meant and still don't. I just threw up the best defense I could think of at the moment."

He made a wry face. "It must have been a dilly. Tom called me after lunch and told me about it. He didn't know whether to laugh or what. I think he was kind of upset."

"Well, should I go undo what I did?"

"Do you want to?"

"No."

"Then don't, but just you remember something, Buster. If you live under their roof, you'll have to take things. I can't sit here like the Oracle and tell you what to take and what not to. That's a decision you'll have to make for yourself. You understand what I'm driving at, boy?"

"Yes sir."

"All right. Go into one of your trances and see what you can see."

I pondered the matter heavily a moment. "I can stay quiet, Matt."

"Good boy. That's the best thing you can do. Do anything they ask within reason. Keep your mouth shut. The temptation to nail them down will be terrific."

"Do you think I did wrong saying what I did?"

"Not if she threatened you. It's past reason to take threats and not stick up for yourself."

"I don't think I ever wanted to talk back to you except sometimes when we're kidding."

"Yes, that's right. You don't talk back." He sighed. "I never lived with anything like this and I don't even know how to think about it.

"Where are we going?" I asked, hoping to change the subject.

"Home to dinner," he said as naturally as though it was really my home.

Dinner at Matt's was like you might expect. At my house it was prim dry roasts cooked to death, mashed potatoes, green peas and a dainty salad. The whole menu followed tediously this unimaginative note. It didn't vary by so much as a green pea from one week to the next.

At Matt's you never knew what was coming. That night it was a great big standing rib roast, cut in pieces over an inch thick, and oozing red juice. Crisp skinned baked potatoes with sour cream and shallot dressing. A huge Roman salad as sharp as Parmesan cheese, anchovies, wine vinegar, garlic and capers could make it. After all that came a piece of fresh cocoanut pie.

CHAPTER FIVE

The remaining few months of that year passed with me watching it at home and at Matt's. I made it a point not to be alone with Ginger and she, remembering the results of that last kiss, stopped playing our little game. Jake recovered and from the day he came home he never said another word to me after his one announcement. He caught me on the back porch one evening, the same evening he came back from the hospital.

"Just a minute, Kingpin," he said shoving me back against the wall. I bounded back with a sudden fury that exploded like hot fire in my brain I struck him in the chest with my left shoulder and slammed him off the porch into the yard.

I calmed a little as I watched him come off the grass. "You take a lot of showing, don't you, Jake?"

He was weak from his stay in the hospital or I believe he'd have taken me on right then and there. He was so furious he was almost blue in the face. He stood up and eyed me with a savage hate that I've never seen in a man's eyes since.

"Okay, Kingpin," he almost whispered. "That's two for you. Mine's coming. Maybe this year, maybe next, maybe ten. I don't know ... but it's coming."

"Make it good," I said lightly, feeling a funny leaden lump in my throat. "And better make it soon because in a year I'll clean your plow like a scrub brush."

I walked off wondering what he'd have said if I'd just stood there and taken his pushing around. The whole thing was beginning to bug me but deep ... but I had Helga.

She was waiting for me like so many times … not always. Helga had business of her own and I often wondered if she didn't have other interests. I never asked because her answer might have been something I didn't want to hear. In short, I was a little afraid of her.

On cold nights we'd cuddle close together listening to the snow hiss against the side of the house or sleet tinkle against the panes.

I guess I could say with truth that I learned about women from her. I never met one who could give more, or had more to give, or gave with less restraint or demand upon me. I was there. That was enough for her. So … I couldn't ask her where she went and what she did.

My best birthday present was a word from Helga as I was going up the stairs to my room. "I have something for you. A present, sort of. Later."

I winked and nodded. My birthday present? My only. No one else mentioned it even but that didn't bother me particularly. I'd never been given a birthday party or had anyone made one over my birthday. Not in this house. Matt and Mamma and Ginger never failed to remember me.

At Christmas I got a few things, mostly clothes that I'd need in the year to come. Such luxuries and foolish things that kids want always came from Matt and Mamma.

"Jackie, I'm going to be married."

She didn't beat around the bush, just dropped it like a brick on my head. I sat suddenly because I couldn't stand up. The walls of her room I could see through a haze of tears, indistinct and muddled. My chest swelled until I thought it'd burst.

"I'm glad, Helga …" Then I caved in and went pure baby. She sat with me on the couch and held me like she had done so many times in the past and like in the past I soon felt better but that was because there wasn't any place to go but up. I had hit bottom hard.

"Who is he?"

"He's got a big plantation between here and Dayton."

"Does he have money?"

"He's very well fixed."

"I could give you some when I'm twenty-one."

She kissed me. "You're a doll, Jackie, but I won't need your money. You're my knight and I knew you'd say something like that."

I was so miserable I could hardly breathe. Helga was my world and she'd held me together for the better part of three years, the latter third being the most wonderful experience of my life. I looked up, hating my red wet eyes. "Then ... it's ... we're ..."

She kissed me and I knew the answer. "It's not for a while, darling. A month maybe. For that month everything will be as it was or better maybe. Sometimes when I didn't let you come to my room it wasn't because I didn't want you but because I wanted you too much. I knew if I stayed on top of this situation ... and one of us had to, then I'd better play it the way I felt it should be."

A surge of elation struck me. "After you're married, could I come out and ..."

She shook her head sadly.

"No. Not afterward. You'll understand that, I'm sure."

I understood.

"I didn't mean that the way it sounded," I told her in a thick aching voice. "It's just that the thought of you being out of reach is such a dirty dose of medicine. I don't have a lot of guts about things like that."

"You have enough with things that count. You're graduating so I timed it just about right."

"You've known all along and you stayed because of me?"

"That's one way of putting it."

All of a sudden I didn't want to talk any more. I wanted to get along with what time I had left. I used it well. And it seemed that her wonderful body became twice so now that I could see the end. There was a frenzy and a yearning that went into our love that I was sure she shared even if she was in love and about to be married.

Then all too suddenly it was the last night and that night I went quietly crazy. She lay on the spread, her arms outstretched and let me make a plaything of her body.

For the first time since I had known her intimately, Helga seemed to lose control. She wept harshly, bitterly after one particularly upsetting crescendo that left us beaten and exhausted. Then finally, when body could stand no more, when emotions were drugged and whipped white with satiety, she said, not looking at me, "Jackie... Her voice was washed out... dead... emotionless. "Jackie, go to your room now. I don't think I could stand waking up and seeing you like we always do."

I dropped my forehead to her shoulder and tried to drive the agony out of my mind.

"Helga ... This night..."

"I know, darling. I know! I was here, too. Don't try to talk about it. It'll only make it harder. Oh God, how hard it is."

"Then you love me a little?"

"I love you a great deal more than a little. That's the trouble. I've seen it coming and tonight you shoved me over the line."

I thought of the overpowering attractions of Ginger and said, "Is it possible to love two people at the same time?"

She nodded slowly. "I'm in that predicament right now but I know what I must do. I'll do it and you must help me."

"After all you've been to me, I couldn't do less, but I'm as gutless as a spaniel where you're concerned. How'll I do it?"

"I'll be gone tomorrow. We mustn't see each other. We mustn't speak. Later when all this fire has burned down a little, come to see us on the plantation. Promise?"

"I promise," and I went to pieces like a mud wall in a hard rain.

Seeing Helga the next day at a distance, seeing her ginning around getting ready to leave and not saying anything to her, was like pulling fish hooks through me. I kept our agreement. She kept it. And of course she'd been right. She was always right.

Two days later I graduated and I guess it could be called another of those days when a lifetime of things happened. I stood an even six feet now and weighed out at a solid one-eighty. I was agile and strong from being a sneak all my life around the house and using trees, rain spouts, ropes and trellises as my means of coming and going.

That morning at breakfast, I can see now, was the beginning. I couldn't see it then, of course, because I didn't have a crystal ball.

Jake, Chaz and Benjy sat side by side across the table from me as always and as always they gave me glares. I ignored them.

Jake started it. "Well, the Kingpin graduates tonight." This to no one in particular.

Mother said nothing.

Benjy said, "Schools must have dropped their standards considerably."

Chaz said, "Yes, anyone can get a diploma these days. Who can ask for more proof?"

"What's on the agenda, Kingpin?" said Jake, "after graduation?"

I gave him a long look and composed my comeback with deliberation of a referee pacing off a fifteen-yard penalty.

"If you don't quit bugging me," I told them singular and plural, "I'm going to come over there and rub your breakfast in your face."

That stopped it but the looks gave me a transient chill. Of one thing I was sure. They were going to fix my plow. I knew it but not having even the foggiest notion of what form it would take, I couldn't think anywhere past the fact itself. That I didn't like. Mother was quiet. In a month I hadn't heard her say a word. She looked thinner and her eyes were sunken and listless.

Ginger had cast some hints about the several proms that were held at the close of the school year but I wasn't the best dancer in the world and I had a lot of other things on my mind.

After all the speeches and the awarding of diplomas and the usual activities, Matt caught me as I came down from the stage and joined the general exodus. "Go home and stash all that junk you have there, you gray headed senior, about to make the world sit up and take notice. I'll drop you and take Ginger and Bert home. Bert's in a tizzy to get home so I'll drop back and pick you up. We're celebrating, sort of."

Mother had given me money to buy a suit some time back. She had also given me a twist-mouthed lecture on my evils and where I was headed. I accepted the money and let the rest slide off me. That was Mother's contribution to my graduation. She didn't attend and neither did the unholy trio. All of which was fine with me.

Ginger was a doll in a dress that fit her like that and when I got out and Matt pulled away, I realized that she'd taken Helga's place in my thoughts for ten whole minutes. It made me frown and tense my muscles because of what seemed a treasonous reaction on my part.

I didn't go through the house. I never did. I always mounted by the back stairs or through the big live oak. I was intending to use the back stairs tonight.

It was black as a pit at the end of the west wing and only a little less so behind the house, so I didn't see them until Benjy had one arm and Chaz the other. I'd had it and I knew it. All of the boys were short, thick and heavy. They weren't professional strong men but they weren't lilies either.

Jake stood up in front of me, carefully out of the way of my feet, his hands on his hips and a diabolical grin on his face. "A graduated Kingpin is still a downy cheeked punk just like an ungraduated Kingpin. I think it's time something was done to sort of change him," and with that he let me have it. Let me point out again that my brothers, though all about five-nine, were big. Jake weighed close to two-twenty. Benjy an easy one-ninety and Chaz about Jake's size. I was slightly over matched.

Jake's left fist slammed me squarely in the mouth and my teeth went through my lips like knives. I didn't go down because Benjy and Chaz held me up. Jake's left slammed me in the rib cage on the right side and I could almost taste the brilliant crack as three of them gave way. A boiling tide of agony rolled up from side and I went as weak as a cat and my belly balled up and spewed. I couldn't feel much anymore... My ribs took all my attention and my head being snapped back and forth by his sledging blows didn't send back much reaction except that it felt like a punching bag. I could hear Benjy begin to scream "My God, Jake... don't kill him... Don't kill him."

Mother having heard and come on the back porch started to scream and second Benjy. Chaz begged in a lower tone. "Jake... Jake, this is enough. Enough, Jake... God, do you want us all to get the chair..."

Jake kept cursing and smashing at me with both hands They dropped me then and I must have fallen half a mile before I struck the grass as soft as sponge rubber. I was a ball of red raging pain, my eyes were full of blood and I couldn't see very well, but I still wasn't out. I blinked hard a few times then saw why they'd dropped me. Matt Palmer had joined battle. Chaz and Benjy were running like scalded cats and Matt was trying his dead level best to tear Jake to bits. He slammed him up against the porch rail with a belt to the guts that drove Jake's breath out with a hoarse bawl that sounded like a branded steer.

Jake's every nerve and muscle told him to bend over but he didn't get far. Matt snapped his head back with a whistling left that smashed his jaws together. It sounded like a milk bottle falling on concrete. Jake started to sag so Matt grabbed him in the shirt front, held him up and tried to disembowel him with gut-churning lefts that'd shake Jake and make his straight yellowish hair pop like a horse's tail. Finally he let Jake loose, stepped back and slashed him across the face with a fist that opened him up to the bone of his cheek like a hatchet.

That was all she wrote, for sure. I could hear Mother screaming and Constable Winters came lumbering around the corner panting. It all got fainter and fainter then silence … silence and night.

When I tried to open my eyes, it scared the pants off me. I couldn't and immediately concluded that Jake had blinded me. The nurse hadn't spoken … she was the silent crusty sort but now she did.

"Black eyes, two of them. Don't worry. They'll go away. Don't try to breathe too deep."

"I did that once," I said in a hushed careful voice. Her warning was superfluous.

"You have visitors," she said.

"Who?" I surely didn't want my brothers around right now. They'd taken care of me rather well and now that I couldn't see, I'd be a sitting duck.

"Mr. and Mrs. Palmer."

"Oh … sure," I said with the relief you can imagine if you've ever been suddenly deprived of your sight, wondering what sort of dragons might be waiting to do you ill.

Matt came in and took my hand and Mamma went around the other side and kissed me. She was crying because some tears fell on my face.

"How is it, boy?" growled Matt. He was gruff because his voice was threatening to go pulpy on him.

"Not bad," I said trying to grin. Brother, was I ever a mess.

"You've got broken ribs," he said. "Both eyes closed and your eyebrows and lips cut all to hell. Your nose is a sight. No teeth lost, I'm happy to announce."

My nose felt like a balloon.

"I'm telling you this so you won't be shocked when you look in the mirror. You're not seriously injured but you look like a bulldozer ran over you. You'll be up and around in no time."

Mamma wasn't talking. I think she was crying and trying not to let me know it.

"Any questions?" asked Matt.

"Yes. How long will I be in here?"

"Maybe a week. Dr. Wheeler is afraid of those ribs. He wants to watch them pretty close for a while."

"Did you catch Chaz and Benjy?"

"No. I didn't chase them. I had an idea that maybe you'd like to have them left whole for your own amusement."

I felt a thick strangling sensation in my throat.

"Thanks. I'm glad you saved them. Where's Jake?"

"About three rooms down the hall from you."

I tried to laugh and that was worse than the deep breath. "Good thing you got there when you did or you might have attended a funeral."

"I have a notion," he said, trying to keep the red rage from his voice, "that Jake has dropped some of his rocks. He was doing his level best to kill you with his bare hands."

There was a small silence during which Mamma made soft nose-blowing noises into her Kleenex.

"Matt..." This was worrying me. "Where do I go from here?"

"To our house, darling," said Mamma and she sat on the bed and gathered me carefully into her arms and held me as tightly as she deemed safe. God, but it was a good comfortable tear jerking feeling. They ran out of my blacked eyes and down into my ears.

"To our house," said Matt in a voice that was so tight it strummed. "To your house from now on."

That jerked more of them. "What about what we talked about on the way home that night?"

"The same thing still goes. You just remember what I told you."

"What did you tell him?" Mamma wanted to know.

"It was man talk," he said so shortly that she didn't pursue the subject.

"Have you talked to … er, anyone about it? I mean about going to your house?"

"I've talked to Tom Morton, the district attorney, and Judge Bernstein. The three of us will talk to your family. This afternoon."

"What time is it?"

"Ten o'clock the day after."

"I'm hungry," I said.

"That's poetic simplicity," said Mamma with a choked chuckle. "Last night I had a porterhouse two inches thick and an oat sack of French fried potatoes all ready for you to come back. I'll see the nurse about getting you something soft."

I grinned, lips or no lips. "Mamma, you'll get me something soft after telling me about that steak?"

"That was a mean jab," she admitted, "but you're in no condition to eat anything solid."

So for the rest of the week I languished sucking gunk through straws and thinking about the porterhouse, gradually getting my sight back and easing more sustaining food into me.

That night Matt and the judge and the D.A. went to see Mother. Matt told me about it.

It must have been an impressive procession. Matt's a procession by himself. Both Tom Morton and Judge Aaron Bernstein are pretty impressive fellows themselves.

Tom Morton is a short, broad, fiery sort with deep blue eyes and a broad mobile face.

The judge is an immensely tall man, a sort of cross between Abraham Lincoln and Bernard Baruch.

Mother met them in the library, stiff and probably frightened. "After last night," she told Matt, her mouth twisted and ugly, "you are no longer welcome here."

"That's not much of a switch," Matt said. "I never was. Mrs. McKnight, allow me to present Tom Morton, the district attorney, and Judge Bernstein."

They bowed but said nothing. "Please be seated," she said, her eyes darting furtively about.

"Where," asked Matt as he said, "are Benjy and Charley?"

"They are in their rooms."

"Will you please summon them. I think it to their interest to hear what is to be said."

She pulled a bell cord and Helga's replacement, a fat good natured colored girl, appeared.

"Agatha, please ask Mr. Charles and Mr. Benjamin to join us in the library."

When she left the room Matt went on. "I have appraised the district attorney and the judge of just what happened last night and on that other occasion you will remember. They have read the medical reports. They are here merely to appraise you of your legal position as of this moment. I am quite at a loss to account for Jake's behavior last night. Nor am I much clearer why the other two were in it as well. Holding an eighteen year old boy ... just barely eighteen, mind you, so that another can beat him like I have never seen a man beaten in my life. It is a minor miracle that he wasn't killed."

Mother started to snuffle into a lace handkerchief. "I don't know ... I don't know. I told them ... I don't know why they acted as they did."

Judge Bernstein was not noted for containment and he had reached his limit. "When they get here," he said with dry implacability, "we'll try to ascertain their object. At the moment I can think of none that would merit such treatment even if he were a dangerous criminal instead of a mere boy."

Mother who had nothing to say wept into her handkerchief until Benjy and Chaz came into the room. Matt said he'd never

---

seen two men who would have rather been some other place as those two. They stopped and looked at the seated men.

Judge Bernstein said, "Please be seated, gentlemen. This shouldn't take long."

They sat, gingerly, and glanced at each other. Benjy was white and jumping from tension. The judge folded his long bony hands over his stomach.

"The question has been posed," Matt told them, "as to why three grown men should attack a boy, two holding him while the other came within an inch of killing him."

Benjy sank back into his chair, his lips trembling. Chaz could talk. "You did the same thing to Jake," he retorted defensively.

Matt nodded. "I sure did and I'd have done the same thing to you two but you ran like whipped dogs. My reason is in the hospital in the form of a brutally beaten boy. We're here to try to determine yours."

Chaz told them. He told them some truths, not all of course, because he had probably never gotten around to the real reasons for their hatred of me.

"You'd have to live with him to know," he said raspily. "Belligerent, impertinent…"

"Not until a couple of years ago," Matt reminded him.

Chaz was stymied. "I never liked him. I never will." It was as close to the truth as he could come.

"I think," said Tom Morton, "that you hate him."

"I do," said Chaz with a certain relish. 'We all hate him, so now what?"

"I might have known that the real reason wouldn't emerge," said Matt. "However, that is unimportant. You haven't told us anything we don't know. The point is, the boy is never coming back to this house."

"I have never hated the boy," said Mother. "By what right do you deprive me of him?"

The judge answered her. "Mrs. McKnight, the deprivation, if indeed it is such, is about the mildest solution we can think of.

"If it comes to that," said Tom Morton, "Matt has agreed to assist me with the prosecution. Actually, it is my choice whether to bring charges. If I do, they will be assault with intent to murder."

"And on my part," said Matt, "remembering a previous assault a couple of years ago, details of which are in possession of Dr. Wheeler, with witnessing by Helga Ehrenberg and other servants, will provide several excellent motives which are in no way related to personal hate."

The judge spoke. "Mr. Palmer has agreed to take the boy. If he is opposed in any manner whatsoever, if you so much as turn a finger to try to stop the procedure, then I shall be personally disappointed if the district attorney does not press charges ... criminal charges. The three of you will be accessories before and after the fact. Jacob will be charged as you have already been informed."

You could look at Tom Morton and see what he'd do.

Matt stood as did the judge and Tom Morton. "That is all we came to say. I'll take Jack to my home. It will be known merely that he prefers to live at my house. What you tell your friends is no concern of mine, but I think you should remember what has been said here tonight. One move on your part to deter me and I can promise you trouble in the largest dose the county can provide."

Benjy came alive. "There won't be any trouble, Mr. Palmer. Believe me there won't. Will there, Charles ... Mother?"

Chaz nodded and Mother crumpled over and wept.

CHAPTER SIX

A week later, I was installed in Matt's house and took my first look in a mirror. I was still black and blue but it wasn't pretty-boy Jack that looked back at me from the glass. I was the ruggedest looking bastard I ever saw. My nose that had been a little on the prominent side had been flattened at the bridge and sort of tilted up at the tip. My eyebrows were thick and ridged with scar tissue which the brows covered, being black and heavy but could not conceal the fact that they'd been worked over in the best fashion. My lips which had been rather sissy and curved were thick and scarred. I scowled at myself and almost ran. Jesus, but I was a savage looking bloke. All of a sudden, I sort of liked my new self. My face would certainly make people think twice before they jumped me.

I shaved the few hairs I'd let grow in the hospital and went down to that steak that had been saved for me.

Mamma ran to me and took me in her arms and cried over my poor battered face. "Just a child and he looks like an ex-convict."

"Oh be quiet," snapped Matt. "Plastic surgery being what it is will bring him back to very nearly his own pretty self in no time at all."

I sat down at the big table made of oak slabs with the bark on the underside and the top side dressed. We were having dinner on the patio. I looked at them for a while and Matt said, "I can hear the gears grinding. It'll come out in a minute."

I grinned at him and winced. My ribs were still as sore as a busted toe. "I got a good look at myself in the mirror. I kind of like it."

"Like it?" said Mamma aghast. "You couldn't. Why it's criminal to let your face stay the way it is, Jackie. Frankly, you're not at all handsome anymore."

"I wasn't going to say so," Matt said, "but I like it, too. You look ten years older, like a man who's been through the mill. If you want to wear your battle scars, then they're yours to wear."

Ginger came in then and cinched it. She hadn't seen me at the hospital because Mamma thought it would embarrass me for her to see me all beat up.

She stopped short, her crinoline underskirt swishing deliciously. "Oh … Jack …" For a long moment she looked at me hard then smiled like a sunrise. "Say, I like you this way. You look less like me and more like a man."

There might have been several ways to take that but I took it as a compliment.

Matt laughed. "Bert, you're outvoted. Looks like his scars stay."

Mamma whimpered. "Oh … you all make me so mad I could spit. His face is ruined and you get some sort of charge out of it."

"His face is not ruined," said Ginger flouncing into a chair and revealing a slice of creamy thigh that made my hide tighten all over me. "He just looks rugged. He could have done with some rugged looks."

Mamma muttered something under her breath and went to the pit to start the steaks.

"Thought of college?" asked Matt presently.

"Yes sir, and I want to play football."

He chuckled. "And you've never played it. You'll have to work at it, boy, but I think you'll have the build for it. I'll bet you've gained twenty pounds in the last two years."

"Twenty-eight pounds to be exact."

"And you're not through growing. Have you thought of anything besides football?"

"I've always wanted to be a sculptor."

Matt didn't answer for a moment. "Didn't you used to keep the place cluttered up with Ivory soap dogs and balsa wood stallions and things?"

"Yes sir. I've played with it since I was nine."

"You should see that nude woman he did out of pink marble," said Ginger with a giggle and I could have strapped her behind. I was proud of my nude which I'd copied from a radiator ornament and I'd lost it.

"Where'd you ever see it?" I asked, my face red.

"You left it at the garden shed one afternoon and I hooked it. It's in my room."

I felt a warm glow that she'd wanted anything I'd ever done bad enough to pinch it. "You need a tanning," I said which wasn't much of a retort.

The dinner we ate that night had lost nothing in the postponement.

In a week's time I'd gained four pounds and was feeling fine except my damn ribs still had to be bound down with an elastic contraption that was a four square annoyance.

One day Matt poked me in the stomach and shook his head. "Getting soft. Talked to Dr. Wheeler today. He says that as soon as you can stand it out of that corset he wants you to swim every day for at least an hour. He says you're all bound up inside with scar tissue that needs stretching. It'll help take away the soreness."

I pondered over that for a while. "I sure hate pools. I guess I could walk to Reddings River. The walk would probably help, too."

"Ginger has announced that she'll be your swimming companion. I told her about what the doctor said."

I looked away. "I'll use the pool."

"Not unless you want to, son."

I shook my head. "I know how you feel about Ginger and me. You're all reasonable and things but you'd rather it wouldn't happen. You don't want it to happen. You've done too much for me. I don't want to get in that position." I faced him. "Matt, for nearly two years Helga and I had a situation that was real gone and way out. I just don't have any starch where a lovely woman is concerned. Ginger is the ripest berry on the vine around here."

He nodded somberly. "I've done a lot of thinking about it. I guess my reasoning is, if it has to be someone, let it be you. You I can depend on. The rest of these pimply chinned jerks around town annoy me by living. If one of them got Ginger in trouble, I'd murder the bastard."

"What if I got her into trouble?"

"If you've got any sense, you won't. I gave you the dope. Why didn't you get Helga in trouble?"

"That was Helga's good head. She knows the ropes, believe me. If Mother would have ever looked in Helga's bathroom cabinet, she'd have fainted ... if she'd known what she was seeing."

He looked at me hard. "You're my boy. You and Jerry. For some reason the affection I had for your dad I transferred to you. He didn't need me. You did. That intensified it."

I nodded, feeling the old choking feeling in my throat. "We've always been frank, Matt."

"That's right. Any complaints?"

"No. I just want to say, if I stay here every day, see Ginger day in and day out ..." I shrugged helplessly. "I can't make any promises."

"Have I asked for any?"

"No sir."

"Then shut up. Actually, I'm hoping you'll be a buffer between my daughter and the males of her set. By and large they're a sad lot and Ginger is all ass and eagerness. She loves to display herself. That's a subconscious something he inherited from Eve. Display and bring the males running. For what? You guess. She flips her tail around all over the place. There's no one here to be impressed but she does it anyhow. It's innate and in women who have a terrific drive in that direction, it's more so. Know why she has that drive?"

"Why?"

"Because I've got it and her mother's got it. I don't fool around with women and I'm probably one of maybe four in town that doesn't. Why? Because my wife has the same drive, she's smart and she can add two and two. I have very serious doubts that there's a woman in ten states who could hold her a light in bed. I like my own bed, that's why I'm in it every night."

Thinking of Mamma I could picture her in the role without any trouble. At thirty-eight she was still a beautiful woman with a terrific figure. Mature, well kept, well fleshed.

"If you want to, you can take the Jeep and y'all can ride out to the camp on Lake Bruin. The water is fine and the camp is yours."

I clenched my fists until they were wet. "Matt, that's just asking for it."

"Asking or denying won't make any difference. Don't you think I thought about all that before I asked you to make your home with us?"

"Sure ... but gosh, doing all that for me ... and ..."

"I'm actually asking you to do something for me. I know how that sounds, what with your early impressions and local attitudes. I just happen to know it's going to happen with someone. The signs can't be that wrong. I'm interposing you between her and the herd. Like I said, you I can trust, the rest I wouldn't trust as far as my nose."

I finally got it and although I didn't more than half believe it, I knew I'd better. Matt didn't talk through his hat.

I found out later how right he was.

Two weeks later I took off the corset and felt fair, although I didn't think I was going to be able to swim the Channel or anything like that but I was anxious to get in shape. I was facing the task of joining the freshman football squad of a major university without ever having played a minute of football in my life.

Swimming in a lake bordered by thick pine woods, to all purposes out of civilization with about as succulent a bit of feminine confectionary as you'll likely see, has any number of built-in hazards. To begin with the suit Ginger wore wasn't much of a suit. It wasn't a Bikini but it was the next thing to it and it looked like it had been applied with careful strokes of an artist's brush. Ginger was now blowing into full exciting womanhood. Her legs were poetry and her waist was a two-hand span. Her hips were round and full and her breasts, while not the magnificent cliffs of Helga's, were excitingly sharp pointed, firm and had that youthful up tilt.

She came from the camp bedroom where she had dressed. I'd dressed in the other bathroom and had beaten her to the porch. She walked with a slight sinuous weave that made my skin pucker and goose up like the hide on a football.

She stopped with me admiring every line of her poetic body, picked up a pine cone and threw it, making me duck and my side knifed me so sharply that I gasped.

"Dammit, I'm still an invalid," I yelled at her and chased her into the water. She struck the smooth surface and slipped through it like a fish with me blundering like a rhino behind her. Maybe she wasn't that good and maybe I wasn't that bad, but I was seeing everything in black and white now. No grey areas.

Ginger liked to display herself, just like Matt had said. She'd catch my shoulders and when I'd pretend I was going to duck her, she'd grab me and hang on, her slick fabulous body glued to mine. Another time she grabbed me about the waist with her legs and leaned backward in the water.

"See, I'm vulnerable.

So … I ducked her.

She punched me in my sore ribs.

"For that you get a tanning," I shouted and started after her. Ginger was fast but I was faster. I couldn't play football but I was a duck in the water. My ribs had me slowed so I didn't get close until she reached shallow water. She was laughing and shrieking, stumbling and falling and finally she fell out of the water onto Matt's artificial beach but I was within grasping distance. She twisted to her back and faced me. Suddenly all the tease and horseplay went out of me in a rush. I fell beside her and took her in my arms. There had to be an explanation so I faked one.

"For that you get a kiss. Just like the one that threw you that night when Matt and I were going to the car."

Suddenly she, too, was sober and there was no resistance. Her arms went about me and the fireworks went off in a brilliant burst of shattering sensation that poured over me. She closed her eyes and offered me the flower of her half opened mouth, then went water weak and seemed almost about to swoon. This time there was nothing threatening and I went to work with a will. Her mouth was hot and wet and soft as taffy and her uneducated but willing little tongue was a darting red snake.

It seems Ginger was born knowing a great many things. For a moment there was a cry from within her that was not a cry at all but more the sound of an escaping overload of emotional steam. There was a blind pointless movement of her body that grew less pointless. For a muscle hardening five seconds she held tense and tight, then collapsed, her head falling back, her eyes glazed and opaque, her lip trembling and her tongue feeling aimlessly about for something it seemed to have lost. Gradually she recovered and looked at me like I was a stranger for a second then a sob came from her throat and she clutched me again and held me.

"Oh … Jack …" She twisted her face deeper into the curve of my neck. "What happened, Jack? Something …" She shuddered violently for a second then relaxed a little. "Something awful." Her wet eyes found mine and held with a strange steadiness. "Or wonderful, only it was …" A shudder claimed her again. "It was so wonderful that it was terrible." I had cause to remember the look in her eyes for a long time. There was a savage sort of flame licking forth from their green depths. I didn't know what it was then. What had happened to her was, I thought, what had happened to me the first afternoon Helga came into my room.

I smoothed her hair away from her damp forehead tasting the silken texture of her young skin with my fingers.

That flame leaped up in her eyes for a rather upsetting moment then died and a smile touched her lips. She hid her face against my neck again and sighed deeply.

"Jack." Her voice was muffled. "The sand is cutting my skin."

"That's because we're wet. Want to shower and change?"

She sat up. "You're not to swim too much at first. I think we'd better."

"We did. She first and I next. As she came out of the bathroom she was so lovely that my heart ached. No lipstick, no make-up. Just clean woman. This made me think of Helga and though Helga was something to think about, I found then and later that what's nearest is dearest.

The sun shone through the bathroom window and silhouetted her to the waist through the light cotton play dress. She'd left off her slip. I wondered what else she'd left off.

She came straight into my arms and tilted her mouth to mine.

Later we went together to the shower and she clung to me as though she was afraid I'd get away. We showered and while still wet the fever began to rise again. It rose and fell and rose again and again until the dimness of the bedroom advertised the setting of the sun.

In the jeep she said, "Wait, Jack...just a moment." She came into my arms and her lips now knowing what a kiss was like made my tired blood come to life, but then she pulled away. Her smile seemed older than ever. "Thanks."

She cuddled up against me and we started to town. After a mile she opened her dress and slipped my hand down the opening and over her right breast. She shuddered, stretched the exciting mound against it then relaxed, holding it snugly in place.

"Take the cut-off," she said with a sigh as I turned the lights on. "The road's a little rough."

"I know but it's a lot more private. I'm afraid a car will come along and make you move your hand." She tilted her head and looked at me. "Jack, I love you."

This I'd been expecting. "I love you, too," I said, pressing my hand to her a little tighter. Naturally we stopped before we got to town.

I was a little alarmed about her fatigue. "I hope you're not this bushed when you get home."

She smiled and stretched like a cat managing to almost climb into my lap. "I won't be unless you make me stop again and run me through that electric... Ooooh..." She had something like a convulsion then started crying.

I stopped the jeep. "Ginger, what's wrong?"

"Nothing," she sobbed. "I just came apart that time. I'm sorry, Jack. I'm not usually such a baby." That I knew and I wasn't a bit comfortable about it. She sighed and jerked to another sob. "I wonder if you know how long I've been thinking about something like this?"

"No, how long?"

"Since I was thirteen. It was always you, Jack. It was never anyone else. I could have many times but I didn't want to with anyone but you."

This was laying it on a little thick because her chances, unless she'd been mighty slick, hadn't been too many.

"I was so glad when they told me you were coming to the house. And do you know what? My room, your room and Jerry's room are all on the second floor."

"Yeah, and Jerry's coming home in a week."

"Oh hell," she said shocking me somewhat. "That's right." She brightened and kissed me explosively in the ear. "But what a week we'll make it."

"Don't your mother and father ever come upstairs?"

"Not since I was a baby … not at night."

"Just the same, I'll be scared stiff."

"Good," she said and I was shocked.

"Come out with something like that again and I'll bounce you good." I looked at her with a hard frown and she wrinkled her adorable nose at me.

"Bounce me," she dared.

Before we got home she had recovered and made me pull off just outside of town and help her into her bra and half-slip. I managed to help a little too well and she fell back across me and pulled my face own to hers. She gave me a long digging kiss that had her nostrils pinching from her labored breathing in no time.

This, I knew, couldn't go on. I forced her to sit erect. "Cut it out. We do have to get home, you know."

She sighed and nodded. "Yes … dammit, but I'll get you tonight." And she did.

The next day I was so sore I could hardly breathe and Mamma put her foot down. No more swimming for three days.

"I knew it was too soon," she told Matt at breakfast the next morning when I came in with enough list to capsize me.

"I didn't notice it at the time," I said. I couldn't look at Matt and I hated myself for it.

I knew he was curious and after breakfast when he cornered me, as I knew he would, I said, "Matt, don't ask me any questions … please."

"Sure, kid," he said gently, putting a huge hand on my shoulders. "Looks like my talk about ethics stuck."

"Maybe I didn't need that part. I couldn't talk about something like that."

It was an hour later before I realized that I'd told him everything he wanted to know.

CHAPTER SEVEN

Jerry Palmer came home and applauded my resolution to try football even though I hadn't played in high school and started in to teach me the rudiments. Between he and Ginger, all that summer was well taken up. Ginger had found what life held for her as regards the shrill high stratas of sensation and I never knew a more finished sensualist in my life. It should have told me something about her just as those disturbing fires I'd seen in her eyes should have told me something.

Jerry had confided to me that he had his eyes on an all-conference spot some day and he didn't want to get out of shape. We did roadwork, we lifted weights at the town gym until I was ready to fall over, but I could feel and see the difference. I weighed one-ninety now and was six-one.

How's he coming?" asked Matt one night after dinner when we were scattered out around the patio sipping creme de menthe after a dinner of baked red-fish.

Jerry who's a lighter counterpart of his father, shrugged his big shoulders. "I'm not happy about him at all."

"Why?"

"Because he has the build for an end and that's my spot. He's faster than me and those weights have put inches on his legs and arms. He weighs a hundred and ninety-two now and by mid-season he'll top two-oh-five, with another inch. Remember, he'll be a soph when I'm an old drooping senior."

I sat up with a snap. "I wouldn't take your spot if they'd give it to me," I said hotly. "Besides, I'll be down on the fourth string and you know it."

They all laughed at me because I took it so seriously.

Jerry said, "If Horvath decides you're better'n me, Bub, he won't ask either of us. I'll go out and you'll go in."

"Oh tie a can on it." I said, trying to hide my annoyance. "Maybe I can scare them to death with this face."

Mamma came to me and sat on the arm of my chair. "Jackie, won't you please have something done about that face?"

Ginger bounded to her feet. "Don't you dare try to get him in that hospital. I'm just tickled to death with his looks."

Jerry looked at me seriously. "Jack, you look older than me except when you smile. Mind you, I like your bruiser's face, too, but you'd better think about it."

"I've already thought about it. It stays." I pulled Mamma down in my lap and kissed her hard. "That's to show I appreciate your interest," I said and released her.

"I'll have to remember what it takes to get that sort of reaction out of you."

Ginger looked daggers at both of us and I just knew Matt was sitting back seeking beneath the surface, feeling the pulses of hidden currents. But, I told myself, he already knows about Ginger and me so what am I worried about? I was just uncomfortable.

We were supposed to go to a show in Dayton my last night at home and we went early so as to have dinner at a fine restaurant in that town but we never got there and never saw the show. We went to a motel and stayed there until the last show would have been over.

As it had been with Helga, the last night was a thing of brilliance and wonder, of the most heart aching beauty, of emotional storms so great that we both became almost ill and I for once was a little alarmed.

It seemed that if I didn't carry a part of her with me I couldn't stand it and she begged me with tears in her eyes to cast cautions to the winds and let her have my child. Somehow, in many ways I wish now I had. Maybe it would have meant a lot of unhappiness for a lot of people and still it might have saved a lot, too. We never know those things because no one can see over the next hill. If there had been any good way out of going to school. I'd have taken it, but I knew I could never face Matt with my reasons.

"Your father had two paid-up educational insurance policies on you, Jack," he said when we had our final chat before I left. I didn't speak and he looked up. "You don't seem interested."

"Okay, Matt. I'm glad of course."

"And by the terms of the will, the bank will let you draw on it within reason to be paid back when you're twenty-one when you come into your half of the estate."

"That's fine."

"What the hell's the matter with you?"

I sat down abruptly. "Matt, having to leave Ginger is killing me."

"I thought something like that. She's been looking like a sick chicken the last few days, too. Do you feel like we can talk about her?"

I eyed him hard. "Only in generalities."

He nodded, "You've done well, Jack. Just exactly what I wanted you to do. I have no complaints."

"Did you foresee this?"

"I did."

"All right. When can I marry her?" This much I could do.

He came right at me. "On your graduation day. That's a promise."

I sighed and sank back in the chair. "Well, that's something."

"What if she won't wait that long?"

"She will. She's mine. I couldn't be wrong about that."

"You could be and if I were you, I'd give that some serious thought. You've been battered around enough in your time so I wouldn't stick my neck out for more."

I looked at him hard. "You know, that's a funny thing for you to say."

"Laugh then."

"You know what I mean."

"You'd better know what I mean." He leaned forward and jabbed my knee with a hard forefinger. "Hasn't this summer taught you what she's like?"

"It's taught me what she's like to me."

"All right. You leave, you're gone for nine months with a few days home for holidays and Christmas. Will she wait for you?" He breathed like a bellows. "Can she wait for you?"

I watched his face for a moment. "You been peeking?"

"I didn't have to peek. I have a mind. I can add simple figures and see through simple people. You'll always be simple and trans-parent because you don't have any deviousness in your makeup. She's too young to be devious, and you still haven't answered my question."

I shook my head. "I can't answer you. You'll have to prove it to me."

"She'll have to do it. Not me! Son, I just don't want to see you hurt and disillusioned. It could happen."

"Matt, why will you talk like this about your own daughter?"

"Because I know her better than anyone else. I can read the signs. I've been reading them a long time. If I'm wrong, then I'll be tickled to death. If I'm not, you stand to catch some bumps." He blew like a porpoise. "Jack, you're a great big overgrown boy. You had a rough childhood and an abnormal one. Remember that. You never had any love life. The fact that what you had was a hell of a lot more profound than a lot of these backroads Romeos ever dreamed of changes little. Helga felt sorry for you and she liked the hell out of you. She was a big fine husky gal with a full set of healthy glands. She felt no more guilt taking your virginity or giving herself to you than Ginger did and if I'm any judge that word has never cropped up in your association with Ginger. I'd use the word amoral for both of them but in both their cases I'd only be able to apply it to sex. Morality is a hell of a lot more than abstaining from fleshly desires. There are some people who are highly successful at abstention. I'm not persuaded that they'd be any good in bed either. You've been roughed up and scarred from the time you were able to walk and I'm not talking about physical scars. I think you rather like the physical ones. With this man-woman business you're still a babe in the woods. If you think I'm being rough on my own daughter, let's just say I don't want to see her rough on one of my sons. Think this over and try to build yourself a philosophy that will enable you to take some bumps. You have some coming. If not with her with someone else. Who knows who you might meet at the University? It might be you who'll want to break it up. You're still wet behind the ears."

"It won't be me," I said positively. "No sir ... not me."

"You're an ass," he said without heat. "I'm forty-two years old and every day I live I'm impressed how stupid I was five years ago. When I was your age I was practically a lame brain compared to now. I fell in and out of love a hundred and seventeen times ... approximately. Out of that bunch I managed to bed a goodly percentage. The real heat came after that happened. It'll do that to you. Tell me, did you ever think you were in love with Helga?"

I was silent so long he said, "Oh ... you knew it."

"Yes, sir," I said miserably.

"Did you miss her after that first trip to the lake?"

I shook my head.

"Now do you see what I mean?"

"I see, Matt. I'd better shut up. I never was a match for you."

CHAPTER EIGHT

This business of school, classes and study took on a new aspect. Luckily, I'd had some excellent high schooling, something I didn't realize at the time it was happening, and now college, though hard, was something like a projection of high school except that no one seemed to care what you did or when ... and harder, of course. I was taking a general course that would some day get me a B. A. sheepskin. There was an art major to be had but I didn't want that. What I wanted was sculpture and just sculpture. That, of course, was impossible so I just took a straight course and hoped to get in a lot of it as an elective.

I suppose I'd have blown onto the campus as just another wind and a pretty good hunk of beef if it hadn't been for my face, but that did it. Men looked at me with respect, men who otherwise might have performed some sort of hazing on me but one look at my face and that impulse died quick. I found that a man who'd haze you unmercifully wouldn't fight you for a mint. It's just yellow coming out in the young. One tried and he wound up with a face nearly as bad as mine.

As soon as I hit the campus ... this was several weeks before school started, since football practice always started early so as to field as good a team as possible by the time school opened, I went to the coach's office. He was talking to two tall, rangy lads with crewcuts, enormous shoulders and tremendous hands. They were ends, I supposed.

Jerry Palmer was supposed to come with me but he was held up for some reason or other so I went alone.

Edmund Horvath, the coach, was seated at the desk. He was a very clean cut man of medium height and didn't weigh over a hundred and seventy-five pounds, but according to what I'd read, he had made the best use of them at Texas University. Seated beside him was a giant of a Polack with a wooden face, hard muscular body, blonde stiff hair and blue eyes. He, I found out later, was the freshman coach. I also found out he was a good one. The two tall boys wound up their business and left.

I stood there. Horvath made some notations on a pad and I looked up. "Sump'n I can do for you, son?" He had a soft mellow drawl that could crack and rise into a screeching falsetto when he was sore.

"Yes sir. I want to play football." He did a sort of double take when he realized that I had a face like a defenseless prize fighter. Modeleski, the frosh coach, looked at me and his bushy brows almost covered his eyes in a scowl.

"Son, what happened to your face?" he asked.

"My brothers beat me half to death once." I said it in a toneless voice.

"Your brothers?"

"Yes sir. Three of them ... when I was still in high school."

"Well, er ... Hummmm. What's your name?"

"John McKnight. I answer to Jack."

Horvath scanned a long roster of some sort. "I don't see your name here."

"No sir. I don't have a scholarship. I've never played football before."

"I like this boy's looks," rumbled Modeleski in a thunderous bass.

Horvath squirmed. "Yes, damn it, but we're fresh out of scholarships. We'll loaded."

"Some'll fall by the way after the first scrimmage," said Modeleski scowling harder. "They always do. They find it takes a hell of a lot more guts to play college ball than it does to run over high schools kids."

"I don't want a scholarship," I said.

Horvath raised black eyebrows. "Oh? You don't?"

"No sir. My father provided for me rather well."

"I take it he's dead."

"Yes sir."

Modeleski looked at me again. "By God I like this kid." He reminded me of Matt Palmer.

Horvath nodded jerkily. "All right. You're in … by that I mean you get a chance."

"Don't," said the freshman coach in his quaking voice, "let the fact that you played no high school ball worry you. I'd rather teach you from scratch. In that way I don't have to unreel you and wind you up again. Are you fast?"

"Yes sir."

"Ever fool around with a ball? Pass, kick … anything like that?"

"Yes sir. I can kick pretty good. I can pass."

He nodded like a lazy elephant. "Well, we'll see."

"Jerry Palmer is a sort of brother," I said. "I live with his family."

That made them sit up. "Hell," said Horvath. "Why didn't you say so. Jerry wrote me about you. Where is he?"

"He got held up."

"Jerry's the best end we have," said the coach. "If he doesn't make All Conference this year and All America next year, I'll eat his headgear."

"Yeah," said Modeleski. "He came as a halfback. He had no breakaway, no jet start. As an end he made it. As a halfback, he just wasn't there."

"I thought ends had to be fast," I said defending Jerry.

"They do but it's a different kind of fast. He has what it takes for end."

I had to learn how to play football just like someone learns to play bridge or any other game.

Modeleski took up a fearful lot of time with me polishing, pushing, drilling and every now and then almost blasting me off the field with his tremendous voice.

Jerry told me about this conversation.

"I'm giving you a boy you'll be proud of next year," said Modeleski to Horvath.

"Who's that?"

" 'Face' McKnight."

Horvath frowned then remembered me. "Sure. I've seen that boy in practice scrimmage. Before the Georgia Tech game when the frosh were running Tech formations he played Buckner and he sure showed up our pass defense weaknesses."

"Buckner never saw the day he could pass like Face."

"I have two good quarterbacks," replied Horvath looking as pleased as punch. "I'll red shirt McKnight and save him."

When I heard this I went to Horvath. "Coach," I began feeling slightly the fool. "You know your business and it's not for me to tell you what to do, but I'm staying here four years. No more."

He didn't like it. "What's the idea? Do you think I'm red shirting you because I don't think you're any good?"

"No sir. If I wasn't any good, I don't think I'd be on the team. It's just that I have my mind made up. I like football but not that well."

"You don't have your eyes on a pro spot?"

"No sir. I think men play pro ball because it's something they like, something they do well and because they need the money."

"Okay, son. I'll play you."

As it turned out, Van Norden broke his leg in the first fall scrimmage and was out for the year. He had to play me.

Just like Matt predicted, the fact that I was in love with Ginger didn't keep me from seeing other girls. Some were frankly shocked and repelled by my face. To others it seemed to hold a fascination. There were more dates than I had time to fill. Some were willing to go all the way. Others were not. I batted about three-ninety which wasn't bad, all things considered.

Christmas, Jerry and I went home. Jerry had to go back because we were in the Orange Bowl that year but he did get to spend a few days and Christmas at home.

Matt and Mamma had let the bars down on Ginger because she was a very poised young woman how and they couldn't hover her forever.

Naturally she'd been dating other boys and we arrived a day earlier than she'd expected. She had a date for that night and would have broken it but I wouldn't let her. She didn't insist and that was the first intimation I had that all wasn't like it had been. I didn't take it too hard because I wasn't the same either.

I thought I'd wait up for her and chose the patio because the night, though cool, wasn't uncomfortable. So I stretched out in a lounge chair and promptly went to sleep. I was in a shadow and they didn't see me so when I woke up it was right in the face of a torrid clench.

Her friend was a nice clean cut kid no different from a lot of other nice clean cut kids. His ideas as to what constituted a clench weren't exactly novel but they were far in advance of his age which couldn't have been a year over Ginger's.

They were pretty close sitting on a rattan couch.

The boy was quite naturally put out that his setup was being kicked in the teeth by a college warrior home for the holidays.

"Why do we have to break everything up because this guy comes home?" he asked hotly.

She cuddled close and gave him her mouth to play with for a moment. "Just for the holidays, Dickie. Then everything will be like always." She shivered and held him close, sliding a leg across his and pulling herself astride him. She kissed him again. "I don't like it either, Dickie," she panted, her body moving sinuously and objectively. "God, what a time we had tonight."

"Me, too," he said in a low voice.

I had to sit there and watch them. I was as tense as a bow string. My hands were sweaty and now I was sore. Good and sore. I forgot that I hadn't been good either. She'd promised and she'd broken it. I wondered how long she'd lasted after I left. I had a fearful impulse to tear this punk limb from limb but reason saved me. She had probably maneuvered the whole thing. In any event she hadn't mounted any resistance. So I sat there and watched them gradually come alive. Heard whispered words of undying love and fealty and smiled grimly as I heard it. Then he left. She watched him out of sight and turned to go into the house.

"Excellent performance," I said from my shadow.

She started and almost screamed. "Jack."

"In the flesh. Who's the hot pants lothario? Not that yours are any cooler. As I say, bonny performance."

She looked at me for a moment then sank back to the couch and wept bitterly. I felt like a heel but the thing had gotten me where I lived and I was as sore as a mashed thumb.

Finally she sat up and looked at me. "All right, so you know. What was I to do? Sit here and die just because you were away?"

"I'd supposed you could wait a while."

"Well, I couldn't. I'm not making any excuses. You hadn't been gone a week…" She looked at me through agonized eyes. "Please try to understand, Jack."

"I'll try," I replied shortly.

She sighed and squeezed her face with her hands. "I just couldn't stand it. I couldn't sleep and I was simply burning down. He was the first and the only one. I stuck to him because he seemed to be safe. He doesn't talk. If I did like I wanted to, I'd have three or four."

I was too concerned to be mad now. "My God, Ginger," I blurted. "Is it that bad?"

"It's that bad. We were supposed to go to a show tonight. We didn't go. We've been making love for four hours. Then what you saw." I could see something like torture in her eyes. "Now I want you."

I got up abruptly. "You won't need to cut him off for two weeks. You'd better call him and tell him because you won't get me."

I walked into the house and left her standing there with a hurt look in her eyes. Marriage? That was unthinkable. Then I thought back and remembered the primordial light in her eyes, the savage flickering of insatiability. I'd wondered about it then. Now I knew.

Naturally Mamma and Matt wondered what was wrong. I moped around and hated every moment of it. I wanted to go back to school but what excuse could I give?

I knew I'd have to tell Matt. What he told Mamma was something else. I'd leave that up to him. So two days later I got the opportunity. It was Friday night and Mamma played bridge that night. Jerry wasn't home and Ginger was on a date.

Matt and I had eaten well on thick T-bone steaks and since the weather was still good we sat on the patio.

"Want to tell me, Jack?"

I nodded. "I've been wanting to tell you. Matt, you were more right about Ginger than you thought."

He nodded slowly. "She's laying this boy, Dickie, every chance she gets, isn't she?"

"Yes. The first night I was back I sat over there by that shrub in the shadow and watched them. Somehow, I don't hold it against her like maybe I should or could. It's a fever with her. She has to have a man. She didn't last a week after I left."

He sighed. "I guess I knew it but I was hoping it wasn't so and that you two could pick up where you left off in August. I suppose it's a job for a psychiatrist."

"I don't think so."

"Why?"

"Because I've been reading about it. Ginger isn't the psychiatrist's idea of a nymph. A nymph never gets what she wants.

Ginger does. She just wants it over and over. If she doesn't get it, it starts gnawing on her and she nearly goes crazy. She told me that much. I'm as sorry as you but I sure don't have any answer."

He shook his head. "I don't either. Keeping her close wouldn't work. Not now. We'll just have to put up with it and hope because if we started clamping down she'd just up and run off with some man. There are plenty of them around who'd jump at the chance. She's a fine looking filly."

"I might as well tell you something else," I said. "I haven't been idle either."

He gave me a strained smile. "Boy, I knew what I was talking about when I told you. I've been over all that myself. Maybe Ginger got a double dose of what Bert and I have so much of."

"Since I was the first one, I feel guilty that maybe I started it all."

"Don't be an ass," he snapped. "You could see it coming. She was as ripe as a hot house plum. You were the first because you were handy. You don't make a person like Ginger. She was born with what she has. Still want to marry her?"

I was quiet for a while. "Would she be any different when we're married?"

"That's something I can't answer."

"Then I'll have to defer my answer."

"Would you marry her right now?"

"No."

"What'll make you change?"

"Ginger could. I'll have to wait and see if she will."

CHAPTER NINE

I went back to school heavy with bitterness and disillusion-ment. I didn't bother Ginger with my feelings because I had half a notion she was having her own troubles. I found that I could do a lot of practice sculpturing at odd times that had nothing to do with the class room because the professor had a lot of outside students and a private class, so every spare moment I wasn't studying, working out with the weights in the gym, or following some likely filly, I spent at Professor Mehle's home where he had a big basement and all the necessities of my choice of art.

The professor, a wispy little man with a Prussian Guard moustache and an accent that was as thick as meringue was a giant in his profession and his efforts brought fabulous prices and a great many of his pieces graced opulent collections, private homes and public buildings.

One of his favorite remarks was when he looked at an exam-ple of it, to nod approvingly, then blandly a students' effort, to nod approvingly, then blandly

I was his boy. I was a stickler for detail in most of my stuff and the only time I got off it was when I wanted not only to make an object but to dramatize it. I did an Arabian stallion, rearing, his head curved to the side, his front feet lashing out, his nostrils dilated and his eyes wild. I made every muscle stand out clean definition and if his attitude was a little too wild and his legs a little too long and his stomach and hind quarters too excitingly carved, it was what I tried to do.

Prof. Mehle looked at it and stroked his chin. "Nice choice of materials. Black marble. Exaggerated, yess, dramatic, yess, arresting, yess. It hass feeling and fire."

The prof didn't pass out compliments broadcast.

At the University I'd become The Face. The sports writers got into the act after my first published picture. I must admit that it was something. I was in a half charge and I looked like I was ready to eat someone alive, a snarl on my scarred lips and my eyes hidden beneath thickened protruding thickets of eyebrows. No one had yet suggested it was an ugly face but it was certainly arresting. Even Professor Mehle wanted to do a bust of me and eventually did it. He, too, exaggerated, making it too hard, too strong but arresting? It was that and more.

Professor Mehle's eighteen year old daughter came back that spring from some finishing school in the East and on the first meeting she fell apart because of what someone had done to my face.

She had an abnormal store of pity for unfortunates, for hurt people, and she immediately picked me as one of the badly hurt.

I denied the whole thing. "Freida, all this happened a hundred years ago, it seems."

Her great blue eyes seemed about to engulf me. "I can see hurt in your eyes, Jack. You may think you've forgotten it, but you haven't. It made scars you can't see. You're a young-old man."

I grinned at her. "You make me young. And thanks for being concerned."

Freida was a slender, milk skinned German princess. Her hair was golden like Helga's and she had Helga's sea blue eyes but in Freida's face they seemed twice as big. Freida's body was of such classic dimensions that it was not a traffic stopper nor was it whistle fodder. Until I saw her one afternoon pressing a dress clad in a tight one piece bathing suit, I hadn't been aware of her body. I Was now and I think she knew it.

I didn't care too much about dating Freida because I was of the opinion that she wouldn't want to play my game and love I'd had enough of. I'd been snake-bitten and was wary of serpents. I had the run now of Professor Mehle's house and though I spent most of my time in the basement, I was welcome to have coffee in the big kitchen and Freida often interrupted me for coffee or cake or something like that. Mehle's wife had been dead several years and Freida, having gotten a stomach full of this posh finishing school, came home and reinstalled herself as her father's housekeeper and entered the University.

I was working on a statuette of John Henry driving steel, in black marble and it was coming out well.

I'd finished it that afternoon about five o'clock and since the professor usually got home about that time on Friday she was making coffee in the kitchen. I was sitting slumped back in a chair frowning at my work, wondering if it was up to my standard or if I should have done anything differently. John Henry was a steel-drivin' man but in my black marble he was a Hercules, muscled like a prize bull with every muscle standing out in sharp dramatic definition.

I guess I was in what you'd call a brown study when she spoke. "Ajax scowls in his tent and the walls of Troy still stand."

I started a little and grinned at her. "Hi."

"It's wonderful, Jack. Really good. Dad says your stuff is exaggerated but that makes it eye-catching."

"He should know about that," I said giving her the eye. She was dressed in short shorts and a shirt that was too small and as a result was pretty full of woman. Her virginal breasts poked at the cloth as though they wanted to come through.

She thumped my dished nose and said, "Come up and have some coffee and chocolate cake. I baked it myself."

I took her hand companionably and together we walked up the steps to the kitchen. My blood was moving at a fast boil when we sat down. The real quality of her had reached me finally and I reacted as per usual.

When we'd finished our coffee and cake, she looked at me seriously. "Am I repulsive?"

I stared at her. "Repulsive? You lost your marbles? You're gorgeous."

"Then where do you dredge up all this distance?"

"I don't follow you."

"You're a liar. I hear you have a great eye for the girls. You've tried your best to be a brother to me. I don't need any. I have three."

I touched one of her slender hands gently. "Freida, I'm afraid of love. I have too much respect for you and your father to take you out for the usual thing."

I held her steady eyes but it wasn't easy. "Why don't you take me out and let me decide?"

So I began taking her out but I didn't lay a hand on her. I kept my distance and before long I saw she didn't care for this attitude either.

One night she made me park by the lake. "I don't dig you, Jack."

"Er ... hunh?"

"So help me if you go into one of your 'I don't get you' kicks, I'm going to slug you. I must be repulsive. You've taken me out three times and you've never even tried to kiss me. Aren't you human?"

"Maybe too much so. You light a fire in my blood, Freida. I'm just trying to play it on the level."

"Suppose you let me take a little of the responsibility."

That seemed like a good idea so I took her into my arms and threw one of my famous ice breaker kisses on her that left her a little weak, starry eyed but well pleased.

"Bravo. Are there more of those?"

"Plenty."

"Let's try another one on for size." We tried on several more and after the last one her eyes were a little wet. I had brought her in close and let her know I was a man all the way.

She stared at me for a moment, her breath stuttering in fits and starts. I started to try on another one. She stopped me.

"No, Jack ... please." She shook herself like a sleep walker trying to awake. "I think I know what you mean now. You were right and I was wrong. I won't bother you again."

That got me way down. "Look, Freida. I don't want you to feel that way. I've got some control."

She put on one of Helga's misty smiles. "I think you have a great deal of control, Jack. I adore you for it. It's just that I'm afraid I don't have as much as I thought I did. Not with the right man anyway."

I cursed inwardly. She touched me on the hand. "I guess you're gnashing your teeth at me. I don't blame you. I started all this, I insist on starting the fire then I can't put it out. I guess I'm a sort of female heel."

I caught her close and my chest swelled until I thought it would burst. I've always loved the touch of hair and soft smooth skin. I stroked her hair and her cheek. I kissed her with brotherly affection. "That's the sort of heel I think you are."

Then she started crying for sure. She clutched my jacket and wept stormily for a moment. When she could control herself again she looked up at me and the poignancy of her face with her great tear wet eyes turned me to water. I held her again and stroked her soft hair, enjoying it as much as the first time.

She pushed away and eyed me for a moment. "Jack," her voice was teardrop soft, "you're a great great man. Believe me ... please believe me. You're really truly great man."

Then I did feel like a dog. I tried to lighten it off. "I'm the football type with a face only a mother could love."

"That's a flat ignoble lie," she said with harsh emphasis. "You're afraid of my kind of love and I'm afraid of yours but I'll remember you all my life. Did you know that for a brief moment you could have had me?"

I nodded. "Yes, I knew."

"You kept on but you played it straight." She subsided and looked thoughtfully at the dash for a while. "You could have but you didn't. I'm having to fight myself to keep from wishing you had."

"Don't do that," I said warningly. "It's for you to decide and you've got to make it right with yourself. Never let yourself get pushed over the edge by something like tonight."

She laughed without mirth. "And to think, just about every time I go out with someone else unless we stay in the lights it's a constant battle for my virtue. The only time I ever really wanted to I'm with a man. Funny how that sounds. Those others went under the rough term of men but ..." She shrugged. "You've given me a new concept of the word."

Again I tried to lighten it. "I'd wanted to do a nude of you in pink quartz. Now look what I've done."

She was silent all the way back to her house, "Why didn't you let me take you to your place?" she asked as I parked under the big porte cochere. We were in the professor's car.

"No. I'd rather it this way. I wouldn't want you driving by yourself at midnight."

She got out and I took her to the side door. She faced me and came into my arms. She seemed comfortable and at home there.

"Thanks for everything, Jack. Thanks especially for being strong when I was weak."

I kissed her gently. "We'll have to take in a show or go to dinner very soon."

"Are you sure you want to?"

"I'm sure."

She started to go and stopped, her face ethereal in the dim light. "Jack ... I'll pose for you." She turned and was gone.

About the middle of the second semester Mother went raving mad. She tried to kill Benjy with a butcher knife but she was just too frail for the job. When they put her in restraint she became very tractable and they released her ... all this was at the house. They hadn't taken her to an institution. Dr. Wheeler thought it was a passing thing, not passing in the sense that she'd eventually get well, but just an episode that would get better before it returned a couple of days later. She made up a pint of lye water and drank it to the last drop. She sort of came apart inside from the terrible dose of caustic and in a few days she was dead.

Matt Palmer came to the campus to see me.

"Do you want to go to her funeral?"

I pondered for some time. "No, Matt, I don't want to go."

"Then don't. Bert said I should make you go. I said if you wanted to go, I'd bring you back with me."

I thought again for a while then nodded. "I guess Mamma knows what she's talking about. If I go nothing will be said. If I don't then tongues will wag. I'll go."

I was sorry I did. I'd never been to but one funeral before … someone I didn't even know but it depressed me. This one did, too. All I got from my brothers were stares of hatred. Later as I was leaving the cemetery, Jake collared me privately.

"I lay a great deal of the blame for this on you," he said evenly. He wasn't much prettier than me now because Matt had scarred him up considerably.

"That's decent of you," I replied.

"I didn't stop you to hear any of your vaunted wit."

"Then why did you?"

"I just want to let you know how we feel. All of us. We feel that you're the cause of mother losing her mind. The cause of her suicide." He breathed deeply and his big shoulders hunched.

I set myself. I hoped he'd try something because right about then I would have maimed him for life and enjoyed it.

"Just wanted you to go away with a little thought. I'll get you, Jackie boy. Maybe next week, maybe next year, maybe ten years from now. I'll get you and don't ever think I won't. Getting you has become my life's ambition. It's the thing I look forward to. It's the thing that makes living good. Everything else is secondary. I'll get you where it'll hurt the most and the longest. I'm going to watch you scream and beg on your knees. I'm going to watch a man became a dog and slobber over my shoes asking for mercy. Take that picture with you, boy." He turned abruptly and walked away. It shook me up considerably and a snicker made me turn. It was Benjy and Chaz. They'd been eavesdropping.

It went all over me like a grass fire in a high wind. Jake would try to get me and in the other two he had willing confederates. With a lunge I smacked into Benjy, blocked him off his feet and sent him flying into a thick hedge of wild rose vines. I grabbed Chaz who turned to run and I ripped his coat from him like it was a "tear-away" football jersey.

It was his fault because he was running with such vehemence … and I never did catch him, but I did kick him in the but just as hard as I could and I thought sure I'd broken his pelvis. He screeched like a scalded cat but he never stopped running.

I walked back to Benjy who was cursing wildly and trying to extricate himself from the fearful thorns on the rose vines. I let him loose as soon as he was free of the vines and the cowardice always just under the surface came out in a pure saffron color now. He turned to run and my shoulder blocked him right back into the vines. Again I pulled him out and this time he set up such a fury of yelling I knew the cops were sure to come but I didn't care. As soon as I had him clear, I tried to tear his head off with a sizzling right hook and back into the vines he went.

This time I did too good a job of it and knocked him almost into the clear on the other side. Matt, missing me at the car, had come back and had seen most of it. When I saw him I was so mad I could have murdered someone and Matt was laughing so hard his face was purple.

"Feel better?" he asked when he could get his breath.

"Much better. You have no idea. Jake just told me he'd get me one way or another sooner or later."

That sobered Matt. "Son, they'll do it or try." He rumpled his heavy hair. God dammit, what do you do about people like that?"

I shrugged but not because I felt shruggy.

CHAPTER TEN

We went on home and thankfully Ginger stayed out of my way. I saw her, spoke to her and kissed her lightly on the forehead. There was a look of hurt deep in her eyes that made me feel choky and guilty but there wasn't anything I could do about it.

"I think," I said carefully, pondering my way along as I went, "I'd like to have a little talk with you and Mamma." That was after dinner and Mamma had already stacked the dishes in the washer.

Matt nodded his big head and called, "Bert, mind joining us in a skull session?"

She didn't but she thoughtfully provided us with a highball apiece that might have served four instead of one. "That'll help," she said as she dropped a gentle hand. "Warms the stomach and loosens the tongue."

I stroked the sweat from my tumbler and wondered how I should start, how I should phrase it. On the way from the cemetery, a horrible thought had gnawed into my mind.

"Nothing," averred Matt, "will loosen his tongue until it gets ready."

"Don't nag the boy," said Mamma lighting a cigarette and taking a seat near me.

I let a gusty sigh go out of me. "I'm worried," I said.

"Yeah," he growled, "and I can't tell you what to do about it. I think those brothers of yours are as cracked as their mother was."

I shrugged the threat of my brothers off again. "It isn't that, Matt."

"What is it then?"

"As far as Benjy, Jake and Chaz are concerned, I think they're respectably nuts ... Mother was for sure. My worry is, what are my chances of inheriting the same thing."

I intercepted a glance that passed between Mamma and Matt. He massaged his big hands together and looked at the flagstones, his jaw muscles jumping thoughtfully.

"I have always said he should see it," Mamma said. "Now I'm certain of it."

Matt looked up and his face was sort of drawn and lined. He nodded wearily. "All right. Go get it. He'll understand when he sees it, that it wasn't an easy decision to make."

"What is it?" I wanted to know ... naturally.

"Something for you to read. It was left with me with instructions never to show it to you unless in my judgment I thought it the thing to do. Bert's right. I should have showed it to you before now."

She came back and handed Matt a heavy manila envelope that had once been sealed by a big blob of red wax. The wax was broken and when he handed it to me, I could see why.

On the envelope was, "To be opened by Matt Palmer after my death." Father's signature was underneath. I opened it and found a short note to Matt. "This letter to my son will explain a great many things to him. I trust you, my old and valued friend, to be the judge of whether he be allowed to read it."

It began prosaically enough, "Dear Son, In what I have to tell you, I make no excuses, I shall seek no justification. This is a letter of explanation, not an attempt to gloss over my past or to seek expiation. You are the child of a wonderful woman and myself. I couldn't marry her because of family and religious differences. To be blunt, you are illegitimate. I married solely to give you a mother and a great deal of care was observed to make it appear that the mother you know is your real one. However, I have now been married to her for five years and I can see the mistake I made. Just how much of a mistake only time will tell. I did what I thought best. I write this in the event that Matt Palmer, at some future date and for some good and sufficient reason, will see that you should know. If I have failed you, I am sorry, but I am only human with the usual compliment of human error. I have done what I could to see that you will be taken care of and this is in the event that Matt should decide it is better that you know what you have just read. In my opinion the only immortality that man can achieve is that of leaving offspring to carry on his name. You are my immortality. It is my fondest hope that you too may achieve your own immortality because it also will be a part of me. Your Father."

I couldn't see. Tears blinded me and dripped from my cheeks like water from a faucet. So I was a bastard. Wasn't that better by far than living a life of wondering if I might not someday flip all over the place and maybe drink a pint of lye? All of a sudden it felt pretty good to know that I was born of a wonderful woman and a wonderful man. What if no words had been spoken by a clergyman or a justice of the peace? A great peace seemed to loosen all my seams and instead of the tears stopping they ran faster than ever. Mamma sat on the edge of my chair and held my head to her breast, stroked my hair and crooned the soft nothings a mother can always think up for a hurt child.

After a while I could speak. "Matt, you and Mamma have done more things for me than I have time to list right now, but this one is the biggest." I sort of choked up again. "I'd like to have known him. You noticed, I'm sure, that there was no apology in that letter."

"If you'd have known him," he said gruffly, "you'd understand better. John never apologized for being human. I was about half drunk one night and I said something to a girl he was with that no gentleman would say in the presence of a lady. He knocked me as cold as a plate of sherbet but he never mentioned it afterward and it never seemed to make any difference between us. It was something I deserved, something I got, and that was the end of it as far as he was concerned."

I looked up in amazement. "He knocked you cold?"

"As cold as an icebox pie," said Mamma. "I was the girl involved."

Matt grinned. "Your dad was a man, son. Never let anyone tell you differently."

I went through spring training with a strange urgency pushing me. I tackled like a maniac and I blocked to kill. The boys didn't take kindly to it and especially the junior and seniors. They tried to rack me up and did but that didn't stop me. Finally Jerry collared me.

"Look, Jack," he said seriously. "Far be it from me to tell an aspiring quarterback to take it easy, but son, you're trying to kill someone. Yourself, maybe. Save it until next season. What gives?"

"I don't know," I said, simply, because I didn't know.

Modeleski was blunter. "You break some good man's leg and end his career as a ball player and you'll have yourself to answer every time you shave. What's got into you, Face? These boys are your teammates, your friends … I hope."

"I'll ease up, Coach. Something's bugging me."

"Like what?"

"I wish I knew. I mean that."

Horvath was cold. "Ambition is a good thing, Face, but you've already given notice that you won't play pro ball and you're here for four years only. You break up some of my men with this killer urge you've been showing and by God, I'll bounce your ass off the squad so fast you won't have time to take off your jockey strap."

That was the clencher and I sort of lost my vapors and played a hard game like a human rather than a one man wave of destruction.

Judd Macmillian, the first string center, came to my room one night about the time I was easing up. I'd blocked him out of play on a pass formation where I lateralled to my right half to confuse the enemy. I blocked him out of play all right but the pass was short and the end did a lot of toe dancing and Judd made a try for him. This time I blocked him for keeps and I really mean I hung one on him. He wasn't looking for it and they had to roll him around some before he could get his wind back.

"That was some block today, Face," he said without preamble. Judd is six-four and weighs a very well spread two-twenty so he doesn't have to carry preambles around with him.

I looked up from the glooms and my face must have been pretty ugly because Jerry Palmer got slowly to his feet as if looking for trouble. "Glad you liked it," I cracked back.

"Such a good block that somehow it was almost personal."

"Take it any way you like," I said getting to my feet.

He looked at me for a moment and shook his head. "You're too eager. If we tangled in this room, where'd you and Jerry sleep for the rest of the term?"

He grinned when he said it and all of a sudden I was sorry. "I got a bug in my neck, Judd. Sorry if I roughed you up."

He nodded. "It's all in the game but it doesn't seem to be a game to you anymore. From linemen I expect it but not from some fancy-dan quarter."

"He's been told about it," said Jerry shortly.

Judd nodded affably. "Just wondered. We'll all be in it together next year, Face. Let's don't start the year with any bruises, hunh?"

"You're right, Judd. I'll try to get myself straight."

Till this day I don't know what it was I was fighting that spring training session.

I'd taken Freida out a few more times. I had my own car now and I wasn't dependent on Professor Mehle's or Jerry Palmer's generosity for transportation. She was content to stay on her side and I didn't push things, although I wanted to mighty badly. Neither of us had mentioned her promise to pose for me in the nude until one night she brought it up. It struck me for a number of reasons. She'd been acting a little peculiarly for Freida who had no particular peculiarities and even on that night I couldn't put my finger on any exact thing. She just seemed upset and maybe nervous.

"You didn't even mean it when you asked me to pose for you that time," she said as we drove under her porte cochere.

"I meant it. You've sort of kept your distance, which I think is a good idea. I wasn't sure whether I should bring it up."

Her hands flew to her face and for a moment I thought she was crying but she wasn't. She'd just covered a blush. "I've been thinking about it. I don't have the nerve, really, but if you asked me I know I would."

"I'd do you," I said thoughtfully, "figurine style about three feet high ... out of pink quartz."

Her eyes seemed luminous in the gloom. "That would, take an awful lot of posing, wouldn't it?" She quivered as she leaned her forehead against my shoulder. "Jack, I couldn't stand a whole lot of it. I just know I couldn't."

"Suppose I take a still shot with a camera and work from that?"

"Could you do that?"

"It isn't easy to some but that's the way I always did my work. Dogs wouldn't stay still so I'd use a picture. I didn't have the nerve to ask a girl to pose for me so I used a radiator ornament from an automobile. Some things I can do from memory. Your father seems to think I'm favored because I can carve from memory."

"He says you're the only real prospect he's had in years. He thinks you'll do great thinks, Jack."

"I hope he's right. There are a million things in my head that I want to do."

A small silence fell between us, then she said, "I could pose tonight. He's not home. He went to Memphis for a few days."

"I have my camera," I said.

"Who develops your stuff? I could get a reputation, you know, if a nude of me was ever circulated through the campus."

"I do it myself over at the journalism school. That's where I took the course in photography. I can do it at night and no one will know."

She clutched my arm with both of hers. "You'll have to help me, Jack. I'm an awful coward."

"Are you sure you want to go through with it?"

"I'm sure but you'll have to make me. Just the thought of parading in front of you in my birthday suit makes my knees all watery."

I helped her out of the car and we walked around to the basement where all the tools and materials were. I turned the lights on and looked at her. Her face seemed cold and yet warm, wooden and yet mobile. She was frightened all right and I couldn't understand why.

"Look, kid, you're trembling like you're cold."

She swallowed and clutching my arms pressed her body close to mine. "I'm not cold, I'm just scared."

"All right. We'll call it off. I don't want to put you through any ordeal."

She tilted her head and gazed at me for a moment. "Jack, how many men do you know who'd duck out on a chance to see me naked?"

I had to think that one over for a while. "Well, let's put it this way. I don't want to put you over any jumps either for physical enjoyment ... of my eyes and my natural urges, or for any artistic vapors I might be feeling at the moment. I have too much real honest affection for you." I caught her to me. "Freida, I like the hell out of you. You build fires like I told you but you're safe. Is that what you're afraid of—that I can't keep my place?"

She shook her head and her golden silky hair danced. "No, that's not what I'm afraid of." She bit her lip. "Maybe it's me I'm afraid of."

"Care to explain that?"

She took a deep breath that moved her breasts against my chest. "Do you know how old I am?"

"No."

"I'm eighteen. In a month or so I'll be nineteen. I'm a mature woman, physically, that is. You're a big clean ugly-handsome man. You build fires, too. I'm arguing with myself, Jack." She lifted her great wet eyes to mine. "I'm really a terrible person."

I smiled and stroked her soft hair. "Are you trying to tell me that you want me?"

She nodded jerkily. "That, of course. I'm just afraid that if I undress for you, I won't be able to stand it. It's hard enough just sitting beside you. It has been ever since that night you kissed me."

"You're a very frank person."

"I have to be. We wouldn't be anything but a mess of crossed purposes if we were anything else. You're honest with me. Why shouldn't I be with you?"

"I think maybe I'd better go to the dormitory."

"I don't want you to go."

"But still you're scared."

"Yes." She slid her hands around my waist. "Please make me not scared."

I had several things to think of. Bed check, but I could depend on Jerry to help me out on that. Should I, after the way Ginger had turned out? If I didn't, wouldn't someone who didn't think as much of her as I did and would maybe get her in trouble? I was confused now and not a little scared myself.

I was a man and she was a woman. I couldn't hope to go through life trying to foresee every eventuality. If I did, I'd get nowhere. I was less confused now. That was the answer. In this game of living, everyone had to take their own chances and make their own adjustments. I'd made a few and I'd make more. At the moment I couldn't think of a better man for Freida than me. She seemed to think so, too, so what was I afraid of?

"All right, Freida," I said with a gentleness that seemed to come from the very bottom. It was the way I felt. "I'll make you not afraid. You've been thinking about disrobing in front, of me, haven't you?"

She shuddered and hid her face in my chest. "Yes. That's what makes it so hard."

"All right. Do you have a heavy robe?"

"Yes."

"Go to your room, take off your clothes, all of them, and put on your robe. Zip it right up to your neck and come back."

"Oh ... Jack." There was a sort of aching despair in her voice. "Will that make it easier?"

"In a way. I'll show you. Actually, there is only one way that you will be able to pose for me without self-consciousness."

"What's that?"

"Do as I say and I'll show you."

There was a couch that models used while posing. It must have come from Germany because I'd never seen anything like it before. It was more like a bed with one end raised and curved. It was upholstered in soft natural leather. I stretched out on it and watched her walk up the steps to the kitchen, her smooth legs glimmering in the dim light. I suddenly felt like a youngster on his first date. My palms were damp and I was jerking inside like salted frog-legs. Presently I could hear the rushing rumble of the old plumbing in the house and I knew she was taking a shower. I tried to put myself in her position facing something totally new, afraid and yet determined. In her way as determined as Ginger. I'd learned a lot from Helga. I'd learned a lot from Ginger. I was to learn plenty from Freida.

She came back clad in a jade green heavy silk robe that could have fit no one but her. Every lovely line and curve of her classic body was revealed as she walked. Her breasts were firm and pointed high, their tips as sharp as nail points.

Twenty feet from me she broke into a run and put her hands over her face. I caught her to keep her from crashing into the couch and she sank to the floor on her knees, sobbing and laughing.

"I'm … simply dying from embarrassment, Jack," she said brokenly. "In this robe I have no secrets at all."

I sat on the couch and lifted her into my arms. She was trembling like a frightened dog but when I cradled her like a baby and held her close for a moment, she quieted.

I caught her chin and pulled her face into position and kissed her like it was to last for all time and wrung a deep sighing moan from so deep within her that it seemed to come from the center of her being. Her mouth grew slack and eagerly accepted my offering treating it with her own. She swung her face from side to side in a perfect agony of joy and when we broke, she went as weak as a kitten and slumped in my arms. I began to stroke the fine lines of her back and the soft narrows of her flanks.

She raised her head and looked at me with wide eyed entreaty. "You were going to show me …?"

I nodded. "I'm going to show you, Freida. There is only one way to take away your embarrassment."

Her eyes widened and at last she knew. She hid her face for a brief time then looked at me again. Her breath was coming in short, sharp gasps. "Jack … I'm so frightfully innocent about some things. I just don't know anything. I won't know what to do …" She began to cry. "Please, Jack, don't hurt me or frighten me …" She went into a hard rigor.

I held her close for a long time saying nothing until at last she had quieted a little. "You were born knowing all you need to know," I said softly. "This is something no one has to learn." I twisted her about and placed her on the couch and before she could become frightened from the move I caught her close and covered her lips with mine. This kiss was a long one that grew into a sort of ravening, devouring thing that was like the opening of the portals of the soul. Her breath was harsh and her hunger something that had been long dammed up.

The zipper at her throat seemed to have ideas of its own and with the movement of her smooth pearly skinned body it slipped farther and farther down until at last I lifted her out of it like lifting a gem from a nest of satin.

"Jack..." Her voice was a throaty whisper so laden with rich repleteness that for a moment I wondered if I hadn't overdone my preliminary tactics. She wriggled closer and held me hard for a moment, her throat and chest so overloaded with surcharged emotions that only thick incoherent sounds came. She went limp and panted like a runner for a moment then kissed me.

"Jack..." her breath was rasping rapidly. "Please make me what you want. I don't... know anything... I've never ..." She went into a shuddering fit again and her starved lips raved over mine.

"I'm scared ... so terribly scared and yet..."

"Yes?"

Her face twisted and her eyes seemed to envelope me. "I'm not ... really scared at all ... Do I sound silly?"

"No."

"Jack..." She made a keening sound that seemed to betoken the end of endurance. "You're so wonderful to me." She lifted wild wet eyes to mine. "I'm not... embarrassed. I don't know what I am. I'm just... coming... to... pieces" She gripped me painfully and went into a fit of wild weeping.

When she quieted I covered her lips with my own and held her with gentle insistence. "I know what it is."

"You do?"

"Yes." I moved and I could feel her grow taut.

Freida didn't give me the peripheral things that Helga and Ginger had given but she gave me woman and until I had taken her offering, I didn't really know the fullness of the word woman. I didn't know the utter exorbitance of giving, the completeness that left me breathless, and while giving she was taking, determined to take everything that was hers. No one ever gave more or took more.

CHAPTER ELEVEN

When I woke all the lights had been turned out but one and we were half covered with a blanket. She was on her elbows studying my face, her thick silky hair tickling my chest and face, the firm chalices of her breasts pressing against my chest.

Her smile was something warm and relaxed and so ineffably sweet that my throat ached and my eyes stung. "I've been looking at you while you slept," she said throatily. "Thinking, thinking what a great man you are. How wise you are and how well you knew and know me. It couldn't have happened any other way, Jack, not and been like this. Nothing can ever again be like this. Other times and other ecstasies but never one like this."

Her body was warm and quiescent against mine.

She kissed me with gentle affection. "Shall we get along with the picture taking? It's three o'clock..." She gasped. "What about your bed check?"

"My friend Jerry'll take care of that all right. I've done it for him."

"About the pictures..."

"Do you want to take pictures right now?"

She shook her head. "No, but I'm being totally selfish. I don't want to take pictures at all."

"I didn't think so. Some day or night soon we'll take pictures. Right now there is a little more newness to dispel."

She cuddled close and folded her hands between us allowing me the entire embrace. "As far as I see, all that has been dispelled is fear. I can't be hurt. I know that now. I'm not embarrassed or ashamed."

"Not even of what happened?"

"Oh no." It came quick and firmly. "Oh no, Jack. Never of what happened." She sighed. "Do you know, few women have remorse who didn't cling to the idea until the last moment that it wouldn't happen. They were stupid or didn't know themselves very well. The first time you kissed me like that, I knew it'd happen. I didn't know when but I knew it would happen and with you. I thought about other men because I'm not unmoved by them. I like men." Her eyes grew serious. "I love you."

"I wish you hadn't said that."

"I know and yet if I asked you the question, what would you have answered?"

"That I love you. As long as you realize that at a time like this love is impossible to avoid, then you're all right."

"I realize it." Her face took on a sad tinge. "Jack, promise me one thing."

"I promise."

"Don't put me out of the running, so to speak, just because of this. I gave myself to you with a completeness that you would find hard to understand. For a while I wasn't even me. I was merely an extension of you. I held you here ... utterly, completely." She made a fearless adorable gesture. "I lost you, dying a little bit with every bit of you I lost."

"If I asked you to marry me right now, would you?"

"Yes. Instantly. Tonight."

"And you won't be hurt if I say that even though the idea would be a great one, I can't even think about it until I graduate."

"I won't be hurt. Not even if you'd said what you didn't say."

"And that is?"

"That something might happen between now and gradua-tion that would make it impossible."

She had me there. It was exactly what I'd been thinking but didn't dare phrase. I was so grateful for her understanding that I kissed her with that peculiar longing that she had experienced twice before. She gave a deep sigh and again she just turned loose all contact with everything and became a part of me.

The semester passed and she remained a part of me. I did the figurine and into it I put everything I had, every bit of imagination and talent. I took time I didn't like to take to make sure that the last tiniest detail was perfect.

I was shaken to the roots by Professor Mehle's remarks. He looked at it a long time and like everyone else who ever saw it he wanted to touch it. He ran his fingers lightly over its flawless surface.

"It is too perfect."

I stared. It wasn't like him. "I supposed a lot of people would think so."

He peered closer. "Her pose, standing on the tiptoes is hard but with the hips and torso at such a severe angle, it is practically impossible."

"Don't the flung back arms and head with the trailing hair balance it off?"

"Yes ... to the eye. Your model had support for this pose."

I blushed. She had had support but I had dubbed it out of the print I worked from.

He fingered his jaw for a long time. "But I like it. It will get raves ... and curses."

"I expect the curses."

He couldn't take his eyes from it. "Her perfection ... it is not like perfection I have seen before. It is like ... like it was a wonderful dream and you got out of bed and did it while still in a fever. Perfection, yes, but emotional perfection. There is something worshipful about it." He turned to me, his mild blue eyes steady and penetrating. "She is not that perfect."

"Who isn't?" I squeaked, swallowing hard.

"Your model, therefore there must have been a great emotional stimulus. From a feeling of emotional perfection comes this dream figure that reflects every bit off it." His eyes softened. "Surely you are not going to tell me it is not Freida."

I hung my head and sat down. He'd read my mail, every line of it.

"Did you think, either of you, that I did not know?"

"We didn't know you knew."

He sighed and sat beside me. "Thank God, it was you and not some scatterbrain with no honor, no sense of responsibility, nothing but an urge to pick fruit. John, will you do something for me?"

"Yes sir."

"Treat her with respect und gentleness.

"How would you know, sir?"

His glance was sharp. "Do you take me for a fool? Moreover, I have talked with Mr. Balmer. He tells me he hopes his own son is as well organized ethically as are you."

Too many people complimented me. Matt Palmer, Modeleski, Freida, Professor Mehle. I just tried to be on the level with people. Was there so few like me? I couldn't feel I deserved any of it.

And so, passed time. I got an appetite for Freida that was like a disease and the way she gave herself to this appetite was the same happy all-giving that I'd experienced that first night. She gave me no trouble, she asked no questions. Summers I missed her like the ache of a tooth and we managed to visit back and forth. She would spend a week with us, then I'd go to her house for a week.

Ginger got worse and got in a nasty car wreck with someone... her latest. No single one satisfied her now. She came out of it with a few scars and no humility. Death's cold breath didn't seem to have much effect.

The second summer she was killed and I think a little of me died with her. There were a number of reasons. She was Matt's and Mamma's only daughter. I still felt guilty about her. Maybe if I'd left her alone… Jerry was crushed and he was my best friend. Mamma was simply laid out and she'd been the only mother I'd known. My eyes were dry and I couldn't seem to shake the tears loose until Helga met me as we drove into the driveway coming back from the cemetery.

Matt helped Mamma into the house. Jerry, his eyes blank, his big body sick and slack, wandered off. Helga and her husband had been at the funeral but I hadn't seen them. I hadn't seen anyone much.

"Jackie," she got out of the car and walked slowly toward me. I could see that she was about ready to have a baby. She was enormous around the middle but the same lovely compassionate Helga. I recall thinking even then, my Lord, but what a busting fine child this will be. It can't help it.

"Jackie… I'm so sorry… and I'm so glad to see you."

That broke the dam and I bawled like a child with a mashed finger. Her husband came and joined us.

"Do you want to tell me, Jackie?" she asked.

"Tell her," said the husband. "She's not just being curious." His voice had an echo like distant thunder. What a wonderful bull for my Helga.

I told them what I knew. Ginger and Walter Price, the local bad boy, drunk and wastrel, were dragging with some other punk and they met a gigantic diesel truck rounding a bend in the road. Price went off a hundred foot cliff and the other boy was ground to hamburger against a sheer rock wall. The truck driver wasn't scratched. Ginger was so badly mangled that they didn't even open the casket which was fine with me. I couldn't have looked at her.

For a solid hour Helga and Hans… his last name was Van Peit, talked to me, obliterating my feelings of guilt where Ginger was concerned.

"That Helga is here, I understand," I said at length, "but Hans, this must be an imposition to you."

He shook his head and showed his even big teeth in a slow smile. "No, I'd wanted to see you ever since the days when I couldn't get Helga to marry me because she was determined to stay until you graduated."

I looked at her through a veil of fresh tears. "I just hope I can deserve how good people have been to me." I turned to Hans. "About all she did was save my life."

His eyes turned a little hard. "I think it's about time you felt the good things. One look at your face would suggest it hasn't always been that way." My face again!

"I guess all the things that hurt are behind me, so to speak. Even this today."

"It's a good thing to put them behind you," she said firmly.

A thought struck me. "Hans, do you and Helga like football?"

"Nuts about it," he said with a grin. "I was tackle at Memphis Teachers myself."

"Then from now on ... for all time and for as long as you want to go, you're my guests. Every home game and every bowl game the University plays in you'll get your tickets." It made me feel good to be able to return some of the good I'd gotten. They were to have permanent possession of them and the bill was to come to me.

It got to be a ritual. The sports writers got hold of it and made a big human interest story out of it. "The Face remembers friends," said one, "and makes a lone trip to the sidelines before every game to give them a wave." By then Face was a name that needed no explaining.

I kept in tip-top shape. I lifted weights, I did road work. I was as trained down as a race horse. I'd learned to fake like a master and block like a madman. In my entire football career I'd had only four passes intercepted

As long as I played up to snuff, I got by with my peculiarities. My senior year I slumped and the scribes tore me apart.

Horvath had me in the office. "You're not good copy any more, Face." He was pretty chilly.

"Do you want good copy or a football player?" I asked.

"I'm beginning to wonder if I have either and don't get flip with me or I'll have the suit off your back. I can do without you, you know."

I got up and I must have looked pretty mean because he looked meaner. "Look, coach. I try to play the game the way you want it. My off hours are mine. I didn't pay for that suit. You can have it tonight if you want it."

He leaned back and looked at me hard. "You big overgrown son of a bitch." Then he grinned. "Face, I wish to hell I could hate your guts. If I kicked you off the team, I'd have to fire Modeleski."

I nodded. I loved the big Polack second only to Matt Palmer. "If you fire him while I'm here, I quit." I smiled when I said it and that ended the interview.

My roommate, Bob Capers, was a big rangy end, two inches taller than me and a few pounds lighter. He tried to find out what was bugging me, why I was in a slump.

"Face, all I ask is that you get the ball somewhere around me. I'll get it. I don't ask for a cinch every time, but you have me stretching for balls just to show the crowd I tried. They're yards away."

"Sure ... sure," I said and went back to my studying.

We muddled our way through half the season undefeated, but I don't know how. Then came the tough one with Ole Miss. Any year you go into a game taking Ole Miss lightly, they'll murder you. They caught me for losses. I overthrew and my faking wouldn't have fooled a one-eyed drunk. In the huddle midway the second quarter, Bob Capers checked signals and I looked at him angrily, ready to give him three kinds of hell. Then Bob slapped me so hard my ears rang for hours.

Someone had the gumption to call time out. Horvath had seen the whole thing and he blew his stack out of the stadium. He jerked Capers instantly. When time was in again I was so mad I couldn't see, so I called an option. We had third and thirteen and

I ignored the play Horvath sent in which was a do or die, down and out pass play.

I was gritting my teeth so hard both ends could hear me even though they were pretty widespread. Gorman, the center, slammed the ball into me, I turned, faked to the fullback who was startled out of his wits, caught a glimpse of his astonished face, whirled and just burst through the line knocking Gorman and the middle linebacker of Ole Miss sprawling. Two halfbacks converged on me but I sidestepped one and barreled into the other head down, churning so hard I could feel the ache of my muscles from my heels all the way to my neck… and then I was free with only a single safety man between me and a sixty yard touchdown run. I did a fool thing and the only reason why I got away with it was because Murdock, the safety, as fast as light and a deadly tackler was looking for my spin shift with which I'd fooled him twice the year before. As it was, I simply ran over him like a tank and it was all mine.

I kicked the point still so mad I was simmering and knocked well-wishers away hard enough to make them grunt and curse.

By now Capers had told Horvath why he'd slapped me and it had certainly worked. Now he was back in the game.

"Sore, Face?"

"I'm going to kill you after the game," I gritted.

"If you keep this up, we'll win the game and I'll get you. Let down again and I'll slap the pee out of you." And they had to separate us again. This time Horvath pulled me and gave me the dressing down of my varsity career and when he was through I was pretty chastened what with the ear that was still ringing.

After the game he hold out his hand. "Sorry, fella, but some-one had to do something."

I was too tired and beat to be sore any more so I shook hands with him and by that night it might never had happened. We went on undefeated and then beat Syracuse in the Sugar Bowl.

The next spring I graduated.

CHAPTER TWELVE

When I turned twenty-one, Matt Palmer had wanted to talk property and the final act of me getting what was mine, but I put it off. Being a property owner didn't attract me, so I said let it ride until I graduated. Now I was going to come face to face with it.

Freida hadn't mentioned marriage again but I was beginning to work myself up to the point. I sort of cringed from it because like anything new, there were several nebulous fears, and the normal single man's backing away from something that was going to change his status for all time. I say all time because I never viewed marriage as a hit and run thing. When I was married, then I wanted to stay that way. I wanted children so I could pal with them and be a father. I was ready to leave for home and I still hadn't mentioned it.

It was the last night with Freida and I still think Professor Mehle took a powder to leave us the house to ourselves.

I went in knocking on the wall of the hallway more to announce my presence than to gain entrance. The door was never locked.

She called out. "Upstairs in my room, Jack. Come on up."

I had the run of the house now and I'd seen her in all stages of dress and undress but I'd never seen her in the bathroom before.

She cracked the door and peered out, her face clean and scrubbed looking. "Come on in and dry my back."

I went in and just as always the slim wonder of her pricked me deep down. She gave me an enormous towel and backed into my arms and let me scrub her dry... dallying occasionally making her jump and laugh. She was unaffected as if I'd been another girl... on the surface I mean. She slid the shower cap off and let her hair fall in a silken wave drowning her cheeks and the upper portion of her neck in a cataract of golden glory. Then she sat before the big misted mirror and began to do little things for herself I couldn't do. I pressed against her from behind and slid my hands under her arms and caught her warmed breasts making her grip my arms and shiver.

She stopped putting on makeup and faced me. "Oh, Jack, take me in your arms..." I already had and I tried to smother her with a kiss that lasted a long time.

She sighed when I released her. "Where were we going tonight? What else, I mean?"

"I had nothing on my mind. Dinner maybe, since I haven't eaten and I know you haven't"

She kissed me and stood up catching me by the hands. "Can't it wait a while?"

"It can." It did. We went into her bedroom and I said like I have said a thousand times there is nothing so fragrant as a clean woman but she managed to be more. She was now a finished artisan and she knew to the millimeter just what excited me, what soothed me, what amused me, what sent me rocketing into joy so great that she had become a fixture in my life.

Twice we decided to go eat and twice things intervened. The third time she said, "We act as though the night will end too soon." She kissed me sweetly. "Let's go eat. My stomach's growling."

I sat on a stool and watched enthralled as she slid into skin fitted white tricot panties, half-slip, the artistry of putting on a bra so that it didn't show a single wrinkle, the slender sheaths of dusky nylons that she slid halfway up her firm satiny thighs.

There's something very exciting about watching a woman dress. Even moreso than watching one undress because so often the latter is accompanied by haste and clothes are tossed off and thrown in a scatter on the floor, chairs, any place.

She was about to put on her dress but she hesitated and came into my arms. "I don't know what's the matter with me, Jack," she sighed. "Somehow I just don't want to go."

I laughed at her. "I'm getting hungry, too."

While we ate big thick steaks and crisp baked potatoes chased with sparkling burgundy I mentioned it. "It's time we brought up that marriage deal again." It took me a long time to get it out but now I was relieved.

She smiled so brilliantly that I almost dropped my glass. "Not yet, Jack."

This was something of a shock. "Why not?"

She reached over and touched my hand. "No one has to tell either of us what love is. We know better than most. You have to go home and talk a lot of dreary business with Matt. Go home. Get your business straight then come back. I'll be waiting and you know what the answer will be."

I didn't realize that I'd had any doubts about her reaction. I must have as relieved as I was when she told me that I knew what the answer would be.

All the way to her house I was in a pink fog. Tonight, as much as it had been already, would be more. A sort of celebration, as it were.

It happened just as I was opening the door to let her out, leaning across her. It exploded right in my face it seemed, smashed the windshield, tore a searing tunnel across my chest and struck Freida just above the heart cutting the big artery. She died in my arms while I tried to gather my scattered wits. Then I went berserk. I raved and roared like a rogue elephant gone mad. I have a vague recollection of people, lots of people, of cops, of bleeding all down the front of my shirt and suit. I was yelling something at them ... I don't know what and I wasn't getting the reaction I wanted. I went stone crazy. I mauled three cops so badly that one of them slashed me over the temple with his gun. Three more joined the fray and I fought them with all the raging fury of an insane man. It took seven of them and a gash in the back of my head four inches long to quiet me. Then darkness, lots of it.

I woke up to white antiseptic quietness and thank God, Mamma was by my bed. I was in pain but pain I didn't ever care about. I started raving again and she had to call a nurse who shot me in the arm with something and I went out again.

It took a week for me to get out of the hospital then it was more cops and questions until I thought my head would burst and finally Matt got me away from them and took me home.

I was like a zombie. I sort of stumbled around in a half-daze but gradually the fog lifted and I learned a few facts. It had been a rifle shot fired by someone standing in the professor's garage door. The way it happened it was hard to tell who he was shooting at. He'd gotten us both but Freida was dead and I knew I'd never live again until I found who did it. Some cop told me that the law would handle it and I gave a laugh so terrible that the man turned white. If I was ugly before, I was hideous now with a new red scar on my left temple all the way to my cheek. I was gaunt, like a scarecrow. I'd lost a lot of weight. I hunched when I walked like I was carrying a heavy load and my clothes hung on me like sacks.

It didn't take long for me to wake up enough to suspect Jake. I hired detectives and they worked long and hard. They couldn't put him on the spot where the murdered stood that night and all they did come up with was that he'd taken a sudden interest in rifles. Had even bought a thirty caliber Remington with a scope sight. That didn't help. We'd been shot by a .303 Enfield, a British piece that could be bought cheap at any sporting goods store. I had every one I could find canvassed but to no end.

Naturally, I had to see Professor Mehle and I did. I just sat there like a zombie and listened while he had a few words to say to me.

"You are suffering. So are the rest of us. I know that you thought of her and I know that she thought off you. This is normal grief." It seemed that every emotion I'd ever had had just dried up and left my mind a dull, dusty plain.

When I left, I had one last word with the old man. "The figurine. Maybe someday I'll have the guts to look at it. Right now I'd like for you to have it."

"I appreciate that. I will keep it for you until you ask for it."

"Never … never show it. I mean not at an exhibit. Understand?"

"I shall never exhibit it nor shall I ever sell it. That is a promise."

For three months, I hung around at Matt's because there wasn't any other place I could stand. Then, suddenly, I couldn't stand it anymore. It wasn't the usual thing. They didn't get on my nerves but I was hurting them. I couldn't stick around and cause more.

After supper one night, I cornered him. "Matt, I've got to go away."

"Where?" he asked with characteristic bluntness. "And," he asked as an after-thought, "why?"

"I think you know why and I won't go into it. I'm supposed to love you and Mamma and what am I doing but making it worse on you?"

"Like some advice?"

"I sure would."

"Ever look at that plantation your father had down in Mississippi?"

"News to me he had one."

"It would be in spite of it being mentioned in your presence along with a lot of other things when we passed that succession."

"Well, I was sort of there and not there … if you know what I mean."

"I know very well what you mean. Right now you're here and not here. How could a guy take so much then cave in when he loses a loved one? Didn't I lose one, too?"

"Sure, and that was my fault, too." I guess it upended me for several reasons. One, it was a full armed backhand that had enough of Matt behind it to practically tear my face off. Two, I wasn't expecting it. Three, I was down to one-ninety from two twenty-six and wasn't my bonny self. I stumbled backward, caught heel and sprawled flat on my back. For one fleeting second a flaming rage poured through my brain but I squelched it so hard it hurt. Matt had hit me. Matt could hit me every time he saw me and I wouldn't raise a hand. In a second he was on his knees hugging my head to his big chest with jarring sobs coming from the bottom. I guess in that one second I saw more of the depth of his affection for me than at any other one time, so I had to make it right.

I managed a laugh and I even managed to make it sound pretty good. "Get off me, you big bastard, before I stomp the chittlins out of you."

That did it and he released me and stood up, his fists clenched, his back to me.

"It's okay," I said quietly, "I deserved it and I got it."

"You didn't deserve it," he choked. "It's just that I'm on edge what with ... Go ahead and stomp me,"

"And get another face full of scars? No thanks, All right. What about the plantation?"

He blew his nose. Pulled a bottle of hundred proof bourbon from the sideboard and lowered it half a pint with one long gurgling gulp. He handed it to me but I didn't do it too good and had to run frantically around looking for a chaser which made him roar with laughter. I guess he was glad of the chance.

"The plantation," he said after we'd taken chairs, "abuts that big artificial lake they made between here and Tupelo on Silver River. Near the town of Silverton. Ring any bells?"

"Vaguely. What goes on it?"

"Blooded Herefords and Santa Gertrudis. You have a manager named Hull who is a son of a bitch but a good manager. A herdsman who is a white man with black skin, B. S. and M. S.

from Southern University and one of the best men at his job I know He has numerous other qualities that Hull doesn't have. I've wanted to can Hull for a long time but he never quite gets me sore enough to do it. You have three thousand acres and a good old home that is modern enough to be comfortable and old enough not to be an eyesore and an annoyance. You have two spring fed creeks on the place and half of it is in pine and hard-wood timber. It is my opinion that you should get away from the scene of sorrows and people who remind you of them."

"But what would I do."

He pondered for a moment. "I'm not sure. You like to sculpt. Go sculpt Kings Royal Master, a Santa Gertrudis bull, that takes shows all over or Ross Hillmann's Pride, a Hereford who outdoes the Royal Master. It's the sculpture done by the mothers carrying the calves that makes champions instead of scrubs. That ought to appeal to you. Get out and learn how to ride. They have horses galore. Ride your acres. Feel like a king and unlimber those bones. Eat Hawkins' mother's cooking and gain weight."

I sighed. "I'm glad you didn't mention women."

"You're a bigger ass than I thought," he said flatly. "It'll take some time but women you need like air and water. There'll be women, never fear."

And there was...

But boy did I ever run into things on the plantation. Jesse Hawkins, a Negro six feet seven inches tall weighing two hundred and thirty pounds of bone muscle and brains was quitting.

Tom Hull may have known his business but he didn't know people. He slashed Hawkins across the face with a swagger stick he carried all the time.

"You do that again and I'll kill you," Hawkins told him quietly and walked away.

I got there just afterward. Hull was in a steaming fury and beside himself with a hatred that stemmed probably from the fact that Hawkins knew more about cattle than Hull ever would.

"No God damned skunk can tell me that and get away with it," he raved after we shook hands and said a few introductory inanities and he told me the story.

"Now let me see." I was already sore because Hull was a fop. His clothes were tailored and he looked too slick. His nails were polished and his handmade boots had cost too much.

"So Hawkins says the price you asked on the bull was too low. Is it?"

"It is not. It's not one of the best bulls. It's virtually a cull. I think two-fifty would be about right for the animal."

"If he's a cull, who'd buy him as a breeder and give you any such price?"

He turned a dull red. "Mr. McKnight, your father hired me and the trustees have seen fit to retain me. I make the decisions. Remember that and we'll get along."

I wasn't in any particular mood to get along with anyone at that moment and after hearing Matt's opinion of the man, I was less so where Hull was concerned.

I looked at him for a long moment. "I'm going to talk to Hawkins," I said without any particular emotion. "I own the place. I've achieved my seniority. It is entirely possible, Mr. Hull, that you won't be around to make any decisions. I plan to make a few myself and in that we might differ considerably."

He went white with rage. "You'd take his part, would you, against me..."

"I don't know. I haven't heard his part. I make it a habit to hear both sides before I make decisions. As for you making the decisions here, I might as well tell you now that as of today I'm the one who makes them final. You can make them as high as the barn, but the final say will be with me."

He licked dry lips. "It sounds like you're asking for my resignation."

"When I do," I assured him, "I'll ask for it. I won't just sound like it."

CHAPTER THRITEEN

I went off to find Hawkins in the kitchen with an elderly lady of color who looked plump and good humored but at the moment she was crying.

"But, Jesse, you been here near onto fifteen years...all that time gone to waste and...Excuse me, sir...?" She looked at me in askance.

"I'm Jack McKnight. I guess you're Aunt Ethel and this is Jesse?"

"My Lordy sakes, boy," she said wiping her eyes with her apron. "You're the spittin' of your daddy..." She caught her breath as she got a better view of my face. It stung her for a moment but she rallied. "Before you got in the wreck."

Jesse laughed with easy assurance. "Mamma's long for the McKnight family. She got me the job here...and now I've lost it."

"Not necessarily," I said shaking hands with them both. Jesse was a terrific man any way you took him, big, gentle eyed but with a placid kind of hell lurking in his startling blue eyes.

"What's this about you wanting a premium for a cull?"

"Cull?" Jesse's snort of derision sounded poisonous. "You look at him and decide. We've been offered six-fifty for him already."

"Then why all this monkey business about him being a cull and a shame to push off on people?"

Jesse's blue eyes flamed brighter. "That's a real good question you have there, Mr. Jack. A real good one. Especially when this same man has bought two other good bulls out of a couple of

Hillman's Pride's sons at a figure that is actually stupid. Pride is nothing but the grand champion of the United States twice in a row. The calf in question isn't but a week old and he'd bring between six hundred and a thousand dollars, depending on a few things."

"Well, that's very interesting. Jesse, can you back any of this up?"

His jaw hardened. "All the way ... every inch of the way. I'll stake my job on it. Just ask any reputable Hereford breeder in the country and he'll tell you the same thing."

I bit my lip reflectively. "And you say it's happened before?"

"With some of the offspring of some of the sons. Never before with any of Pride's."

"And being offspring of the lesser bulls, you didn't argue the point?"

"I argued it. I was told to mind my own business."

Aunt Ethel poured me a cup of coffee. "Here, boy. Drink this. It's good for what ails you and looks like you're the old man come back."

"It's decent of you to take my part," said Jesse haltingly, "but I don't work under any man whose only answer to logic is a slash across the face with a swagger stick."

I could feel the steam rising out of my collar. "I've just stepped across the threshold, Jesse. I can't say for certain what I'll do about this, but I've already locked horns with Mr. Hull. It's possible that he isn't here for long. Will you consider staying and say you're working for me?"

Jesse took a chair and I sipped a cup of the best coffee I ever drank.

He sighed heavily. "That's a load off my back. My children were born here. I was born here. Mamma and Pappa were born here. It's the only home I ever knew. I think you and I can get along."

" 'Course you can," snapped Aunt Ethel shoving a smoking hot something on my plate. "He's a Mc-Knight, ain't he?"

That was that for the time being, at least, and I went back into the house to unpack. Voices from the broad veranda stopped me.

One was mellow, soft, a caress even in anger. "I've seen all I want to of you, Tom, as I've told you before. I understand the owner is here. He's the one I want to see."

"He'll do what I tell him," snarled Hull in a voice so ill-tempered that I could have swatted him.

I walked out on the porch and made the mental note that beautiful women seemed to cross my trail without the slightest effort on my part.

"Good afternoon," I said watching her start, watching a flit of fear strike her face seasoned with disappointment. "I'm John McKnight."

"How do you do," she was at a loss. She'd wanted to see the master but now she wasn't so sure. She had a slim straight body, strong and very active or I was no judge. Like Freida in some ways, like Ginger in some ways, like herself in too many ways to enumerate. She wore neatly pressed jeans that were skin fitted... to her embarrassment, I later discovered but she hadn't intended coming. It was done on the impulse of the moment. She wore a white silk shirt and a light jacket, the weather being cool. The conical leap of her breasts held the jacket together... like they had thrust themselves partly through the corduroy and though it was not buttoned it couldn't pull away from them. They were restrained by some wisp of a gesture but it could be seen that they were a little too lightly covered for her to risk taking off her jacket.

"You wanted to see me?" I prompted.

"Yes..."

"Oh hell," Hull interrupted harshly. "She and her old man has been wanting to lease the shoreline from us. The shoreline of the lake so they can put up some more cabins. I've told them any number of times we couldn't allow it."

Her face was a thing of such pristine purity that one might have gotten the impression of artificiality but it could never be that. Her skin was cream smooth with lips I'll have to describe later. Her nose was patrician but not severe and her eyes were a melting deep blue shaded by luxuriant coppery lashes. Her hair was cut medium short and seemed to wave naturally and being very fine had an air of delightful disorder about it.

The eyes narrowed at his interruption. "I remember when you didn't think it was so impossible," her voice was low and furious.

Suddenly remembering her first words, a great light struck me. Here was a swain who'd been put in his place and it had bruised his manhood in a manner that he hadn't enjoyed and probably couldn't forgive.

I grinned and when I grin my face is a great deal more acceptable. "Miss, did you ever slap our boy Hull here?"

Her eyes flamed. "No, I didn't slap him. I opened his head with the barrel of a thirty-eight special. They had to take ten stitches in it."

Something about the whole thing, the poetic justice of it, the fact that I disliked Hull intensely ... all of this amused me and I roared with laughter. Hull's rather effeminate face flamed red and he puffed like an adder.

"If she'd been a man ..."

"If I'd been a man, I'd have killed you," she spat with venom.

Her chest was heaving with rage and the result made me like Hull even less. I could see him trying to get fresh with this lovely creature and I was glad she'd split his head.

"I'll get you yet ... bitch," he bit off so mad he couldn't see. I could and I did my very best to slap his teeth down his throat. The blow slammed him back against the wall with a thud and as he bounced I grabbed him and screwed his shirt front up into a tight ball and pulling him to his tiptoes I looked into his purpling face at close range.

"Get off this place tonight," I said with soft malice. "If you have any time coming, see Matt Palmer, but don't come back here."

"My day will come," he said hoarsely. "My day … for both of you and you'll remember it."

I grabbed him from the floor and got another twist in his shirt. "I think the lady has an apology coming. Make it fast and sincere, Buster."

"I'll see you both in hell first." He could barely get it out and when he did I cut all his air off until his face was a nice shade of blue and his eyes looked about ready to pop from their sockets.

"Ready to talk?" I said and let him breathe. He took his time recovering but it took two more airless sessions before he could get out any sort of apology. When he did I shoved him away.

"All right, go get your stuff together and beat it."

"I can't get my stuff together in a short time," he blazed futilely. "I've been here longer than a week."

"Send for it. Don't let me see your face around here again."

When he had gone I got sick. I was weak and had been riding the shrill heady adrenalin of a man in a gallant fury. I sat suddenly and wiped a quick deposit of sweat from my face.

She dropped to her knees beside my chair. "Oh, Mr. McKnight … you're ill … you shouldn't have … He'll make a fearful enemy."

"I've made a few," was all I could think of to say. I was beginning to feel better. "I didn't get your name."

"Oh … I'm Laurie Stewart. We own Lake Nedderville. My father had it built and had a verbal agreement with your father about your part of the shoreline. He couldn't prove it and Mr. Hull has been very nasty about it … after our disagreement."

"I take it he was nasty which led to the disagreement."

She stood up suddenly. "You can't possibly imagine how nasty." She shuddered, her lips turned white and she leaned back against a fat column to regain her balance.

"I'm sorry," I said getting up and catching her arms. "I didn't know it was that bad."

She shook her head until her hair danced. "No one knows, really." Suddenly she looked up and caught her breath. "My God, what am I saying?"

"Some people have found me easy to talk to," I said gently.

"I'm sorry," she said stiffly. "I'll go now."

"But you haven't asked me about the shoreline?"

She took in a shuddering sigh. "I know. I shouldn't have come." She looked down at herself in quick embarrassment. "I wasn't even dressed for it. I can come back or ..." Her eyes lighted. "You can come to dinner some night and meet my father and mother. You'll love them."

"If you're a sample, then I'm sure I will. Actually, I know nothing about the shoreline. I haven't seen it. Maybe Hull's right." This was a fishing effort.

Her lips tightened. "One of the reasons why Dad built the lake was that your father promised to give him a lease on the shoreline. Dad's no business man. He drew up a paper and your father signed it ... for the lake bottom. Stupidly Dad forgot to include the shoreline. As it is, we only have about half of it. We've never been able to develop the place like it should be. Dad's supporters are not happy at all about the return on their money."

"Why didn't your father go to Matt Palmer?"

"He says Mr. Palmer is a lawyer and very businesslike. He'd want proof, too."

"But I can't see why your father couldn't have negotiated a lease. How much land does he want?"

"Any amount you'll be willing to let us have. You see we build camps and rent them. Anything big enough to put a camp on in a strip around the shoreline. Dad had agreed with your father that he'd leave corridors for your cattle to drink and the amount in acreage for the camps would be negligible." Her face lit up with eagerness. "Please say you'll come to dinner and talk to Dad."

I caught her eyes with mine and for the first time since Freida's death I could feel some life coming back. She flushed a little at my direct gaze and looked away.

"I'll come," I said in a voice that deepened the flush.

After supper Jesse came to the front door. "Helped Mamma with the dishes and she's gone. Wondered if you'd mind if I sat and talked a while?"

"I'd mind if you didn't. How'd you like a drink?"

I could see his brilliant teeth gleam in the starlight. "Tickled pink. Tell me where and I'll serve."

"There's a couple of fifths in my valise. Bring some ice and water."

"I'll have a Coke with mine if it's all right with you."

"Sure. Anything you want."

We sat and drank and he brought me up generally on the breeding efforts of the plantation. Seemed like we were quite the stuff with our blood lines that he'd helped get started and had watched so carefully. Our lines were nationally famous and we had won all sorts of trophies. He had a job, too. Just the book-work would have thrown me.

"Starting tomorrow, you sell what and when and at what price you choose," I told him. "I know nothing about such things. And starting tomorrow, you get a raise commensurate with your work and responsibility. In other words, you'll not only be herds-man but major domo as well ... unless it's too much to handle."

He chuckled. "Many a breeder does all his own managing. I can point my finger with the best."

"Tell me about the Stewarts."

"Good people. The best."

"Would Mr. Stewart lie about having had a verbal agreement with my father about that shoreline?"

"No sir. Mr. Stewart isn't that sort as you'll see. He doesn't have to lie."

"And the daughter?"

He shrugged his big shoulders. "I know little of her. She's a nice lady. She doesn't think that Negroes are dirt. She's fair, she's civil and she doesn't ride her position. That's all I ask of any white person."

"Then I take it, this nationwide agitation you want no part of?"

"You may so take it. I've been north and it sickens me. I was made over a lot because I was a hell of a basketball and football player in my day. I was made over because I was a member of a downtrodden minority. Funny... no one ever trod on me. No one with any obvious quality ever made over me for any reason. Compliments, yes. I got myself an education, I can do a job, I have a job and I'm very happy with it. I get along with anyone who wants to get along."

"Didn't Hull tread on you?"

"Not successfully. He struck me, if you want to put that on record, and I didn't strike back I felt deep down that it is bigger to accept a blow from a small person than to give one. I'm here and I still have my job. Where's he?"

"I see what you mean. Jesse, we'll get along."

"I never doubted it for a moment. Mamma wouldn't let me. You know, she predicted this arrival of yours."

I sat up. "The hell she did? I didn't know myself that I was coming until a few days ago."

"Well, Mamma knew years ago. She'd say, 'Wait till my boy gets home. He'll make things hop.' Guess you did, at that."

Things had hopped all right. Everything jumped at me right off the bat and I started swinging.

Next day I let Rex, the big sorrel stallion, take me on a ride to the lake.

I followed the creek to where it entered the northern extremity of the lake and I could then see what a tremendous job Stewart had done. He had chosen a point where the creek had flowed between two sharp hills and had simply bulldozed half of each into the creek and made a lake which covered a good five thousand acres. Far to the south and directly across from me I could see where he had built rustic log cabins with boat docks for each one. From all I could see even in the middle of the week he had a pretty full house. Four speed boats were tearing about pulling water skiers and any number of smaller boats were dotted about the shoreline in protected nooks fishing.

I put Rex into a fast running walk and moved southward toward the main clubhouse, utilizing a path made by cattle, the grade herd that was pastured in the woods.

CHAPTER FOURTEEN

The clubhouse was a sprawling rustic affair with hand split oak shingles and finished in rough sawed wood. There was a restaurant, dancing space and a bar that served ice and soft drinks. As elsewhere in dry but liquor taxed Mississippi, your whiskey bottle was your own affair but no one minded serving you setups.

I went to the main office and found a woman seated behind the desk that gave me a mild shock. She was a twin for Laurie, with the same hairdo, not a grey strand in it, with a wonderful figure that showed maturity but was the richer for it. She had to be Laurie's sister.

"Good afternoon," I said taking off my white Stetson. "I'm looking for the Stewarts."

She smiled and I could see that her lips were the same smooth lush lips I'd been so intrigued with when I first saw Laurie.

"I'm Mrs. Stewart..." She got a good look at my face and sort of withdrew.

I gave her my best smile. "I frighten children, dogs, and young girls. I'm sorry if I startled you."

She stood up. "You didn't... I was just..." She shrugged. "All of a sudden I wondered what had happened to you. I didn't mean to be so obvious."

"People do that... have been for so long it doesn't bother me anymore. I'm John McKnight. You say you're Mrs. Stewart?"

"Yes. I'll get my husband." She gave me a slender well-kept hand. "We're very glad to meet you, Mr. McKnight. Laurie told us of her meeting with you."

"We?" I tossed an eyebrow.

She laughed freely. "Yes, we. Stoney, that's my husband, short for Stonewall, has been hoping you'd call. I'll get him, he's out back repairing a boat."

"Maybe it'd be better if I went out back. Then he could continue with the boat and we could talk without his wasting time."

"Oh no. We'll have coffee here in the office. I want to be in on this talk, too."

Stonewall Jackson Stewart didn't look much like a businessman. He was fiberglassing a boat bottom and though I'm sure he was doing a good job, he was dressed in faultless khakis that fitted his tall muscular broad shouldered body like they'd been tailored. Not a speck of muss was detectable. He took off gloves and straightened up as we approached. We were introduced and his grip almost lifted me to my toes.

"Just at a spot where I can quit. Needs sanding again now. Come on and let's have coffee."

Stewart looked forty-five. I later found out he was fifty-five. His hair was snow white but his skin looked like it had been cured by tropical sun to the color of fine tan leather. He wore a severely symmetrical moustache, also white, and his eyebrows were thicker than Matt Palmer's but they, oddly enough, were as black as the wing of a crow. His face was sharply planed and angled without seeming long or cadaverous.

Mrs. Stewart served coffee in slim demi-tasse cups as people do who drink a lot of coffee, strong coffee ... and it was strong.

I took a sip and faced him. "I think we should get business over then rise to better things."

His blue eyes twinkled. "A capital idea. I like a man who goes to the heart of things."

"You say my father gave you a verbal promise that he'd lease you the shoreline of the lake?"

"That is absolutely correct. I won't support the assertion any stronger than that."

"That's enough for me. If you'll get your lawyer to draw up the papers, I'll sign them."

He almost dropped the cup. "You mean ... just like that?"

"How did it happen that you didn't include that in the original agreement?"

"Because," said his wife, "he's the world's worst businessman. He's a retired Major who knows everything about how to deploy troops, make flanking movements, set up security on the march and things like that. There's even some question as to the validity of the original paper that only took care of the lake bottom. He didn't think a lawyer was necessary."

Mr. Stewart sighed. "I'm the sort of fool who thinks that an agreement between gentlemen is as good as a contract drawn up by a battery of lawyers. It seems I was mistaken and of course neither I nor your father could foresee death. As for the oversight, it was one of those unspoken things ... You know, like what use is the lake bottom to me if I can't have use of the shoreline? The company owned the rest of the land but a good third to a half of it is on your land."

"Well, that part of your problem is over. Did you see Matt Palmer about the paper my father signed?"

"Yes I did, and it happens that Mr. Palmer knew of the deal first hand therefore he was willing as a trustee to go along with it. I approached him after Hull suggested that not even that paper was any good."

"Why didn't you approach Matt about the lease?"

Stewart shrugged. "To be perfectly frank with you, I intended to but my time and money was taken up getting such shoreline as I had access to in order, building cabins and the like. Then after I talked with Hull about the shoreline, he convinced me that the trustees would take his word that it was economically unsound for the plantation."

"Hull wasn't so all fired hard to get along with at one time, was he?"

Stewart stiffened and I saw Mrs. Stewart's hands clench. "How," he asked, "did you know that?"

"I found Laurie talking to Hull on my front veranda. A few sparks flew and I think she told me more than she would have considered wise in other circumstances. Let me assure you that you have my sympathy, that I think Laurie is a very fine person and I'm not a person who runs off at the mouth."

Mrs. Stewart's hands unclenched and her husband slumped a little then stood up. "You'll stay to supper, of course?"

"I hadn't thought of it this soon. Laurie invited me, but ..."

"It's settled." He got up. "Son, you stay here and talk to Eadie while I finish that last coat on the boat. Laurie'll be back in a moment. She's in town right now doing a few errands." He turned to go, then stopped. "By the way, I'm going to call you Jack."

"I'd like that, sir."

"Well, what do you know about Hull?"

"Nothing really."

"Then watch him. He's the sort who'll do you real dirt just so long as he's in no danger."

Then he left and it struck me with considerable force that I'd completely forgotten about my brothers, Jake in particular. I guess I sat down rather abruptly and looked detached, so to speak, but now that I had thought of Jake my back was crawling.

"You thought of something?" asked Mrs. Stewart.

I grinned wryly. "Yes. Mr. Stewart reminded me that the brother who gave me this face made a solemn vow to kill me ... or as he put it 'to get' me. It had slipped my mind and although I don't live in fear of him, I think I'd be stupid to take the attitude that he wouldn't. He's like Hull. He'd do it today if he thought he could get away with it."

She came around in front of me and stopped, her face troubled. "You say a brother did this to you?"

"Well, not really. I went along for most of my life thinking they were half-brothers. Not too long ago I discovered they weren't any relationship at all."

"They?"

"There are three of them. Two of them held me while Jake worked my face over. This other scar here is where a policeman hit me during a momentary insanity that struck me when the girl I was engaged to was killed as we sat in my car under her car-port."

She came closer and touched my face with gentle hands, caressing the scars and making that old stuffy sick feeling rise to my throat when people, particularly women, are genuinely kind to me.

"I'm so very sorry," she said with a mother's gentleness. I clenched my jaws and kept back tears that wanted to come the worst way.

"Thank you," I said and it came out without much life. "Mrs. Stewart, I heard the story about Laurie and Hull. At least what my breeder knew. Did it leave a scar on her?"

"I'm afraid so, son," she said softly. "I'm afraid so. When she came back from your place last night she was sparkling with such a fierce brilliance that I was really elated for a time that maybe you could raise her from the glooms. I very stupidly said something to the effect that you must be some man to make her take on so and she withdrew instantly into her shell."

"But she did come out of it for a while?"

"Oh yes. Are you attracted to her, Jack?"

"I don't think I was ever more attracted to anyone on such short acquaintance but I'm afraid, too, Mrs. Stewart."

"Why?"

"Two of the only three girls I ever loved came to early terrible deaths. I can't submit Laurie to this danger."

She was silent for so long that I raised my eyes. She was looking at me fixedly. "Surely you don't believe that?" It wasn't as devastating as Matt Palmer's backhand but the way she said it was impressive enough.

"You don't understand. I've gotten over the superstitious part but if Jake ever suspected that she meant anything to me, it's possible he'd work on me through her. It's a danger I can't afford to chance."

She heaved a sigh that somehow didn't convey a heavy load. It was almost a sigh of relief. "Now let me tell you something. You and this family are going to be friends...good friends. You've already done your part helping us about that shoreline. Laurie is not a usual girl. She's very strong, she can shoot a gun and pistol better than her father and she's tough minded. Stoney is first and last a military man. He's making a go here because he likes it and the location is perfect. It took all the persuasion and salesmanship I could muster to keep him from killing Tom Hull. He was simply berserk. Right now, Tom won't ever meet him on the street. Before I could get to him that night, he stood in your front yard and called Tom every awful thing he could lay his tongue to. He had a service forty-five in his hand and if Tom'd shown his face, he'd been a dead man. We learned later that he'd sneaked out of the back of the house, caught a horse and ridden off into the woods. He was hard to find for two months."

I frowned. "It's peculiar that we never heard of this."

"Not so much. Very few people knew. The Negroes, naturally, but Negroes may talk a great deal among themselves about white people but rarely to a white person."

"Yes, Jesse didn't want to tell me what he knew."

She frowned and sat down. "Sometimes I have the feeling that I don't even know it all. I know what she told me but I've had the feeling a long time that she didn't tell me everything."

"You haven't pushed matters, I take it. I mean like trying to pin her down."

"Oh no. I didn't think that a good idea and at the same time if things did happen worse than we thought, my fear is that she's loaded with a lot of mental driftwood that would better be aired. People can work up some fine fixations incubating thoughts of their own production, never letting them be ventilated. No one is completely self-sufficient mentally. So many things become clearer upon discussion. Some things even change entirely."

I stood up. "Mrs. Stewart, I've been riding all day. I'm sweaty and dusty. I'll run home and shower and change and drive back."

She got up and laid her hands on my arms. "Your face did shock me, Jack," she said softly. "Now all I see in it is quiet strength, a strength that is touched with gentleness and understanding. You've been through a lot... oh we've heard of you in round about ways and we watched you play football times on end. I think the fact that you've been through a lot makes you understanding and gentle, that and the fact that you're big and strong and could hurt so easily."

I nodded. "Perhaps you're right. All I know is I never wanted to hurt anyone except one space of time after Mother committed suicide and I had a brush with my brothers. I saw an enemy in every man and got very sorely taken down about it. It ended and never happened again."

"I have an idea," she said after a slight pause. "Wait until Laurie comes back and let her run you home and bring you back."

"But I have a horse..."

She smiled, making me see Laurie's wonderful lips again. "Let's do it my way. I'll have Murdock, he's the handy man, ride your horse home. Y'all can bring him back when she takes you home."

I studied it out for a moment. "Why all this?"

"I want you and Laurie to have association. Let it be accidental like for the first few times. If you think a lot of her... if you come to think more, you're going to have some rough roads to travel. I very much fear that she has some sort of fixation against sex as a result of her experience with Tom Hull." She came close and fastened me with her deep blue eyes. "Jack, there can be sex without love but there can be no love without sex, not the sort of love I want you to have for my daughter."

"This is all pretty fast, Mrs. Stewart. I've seen her once."

"Yes, and I venture the guess that she shook you to your toenails."

I grinned. "You're sure right there, but why this whole hearted acceptance of me?"

She sighed and looked away. "Maybe I'm like Stoney. Maybe I'm too impulsive. Maybe I just want my daughter's happiness so badly that I can't see anything else. I've said before it's not like you're a stranger. Before you could remember, your father spoke of you."

"Did he hint as to who my mother might be?"

"Yes, Jack."

I was stunned for a moment. "Then you know?"

"Yes. I know."

"And the circumstances?"

"And the circumstances."

"You're still willing for your daughter to associate with me knowing I'm a bastard?"

For a moment I thought she was going to slap me. "Don't ever say that again," she said with deadly softness. "Not ever … do you hear?"

"Yes ma'am."

"All right. I hear Laurie coming now."

"But … will you tell me …?"

"The secret is not mine alone, son. I can't make you a promise. Maybe, maybe not."

"Then she's still alive?"

"She's alive."

"Nearby?"

"Near enough."

"Is she all right? I mean is she in want? Is she getting on well?"

She smiled. "Son, you should know your father better than that. He made very sure that she'd never be in want. Now let's go see Laurie."

Laurie was dressed in slacks. The tight jeans she wore in semi-private she never wore to town or in company for the simple reason that she filled them a little too excitingly for the general public. She was wearing a light summer weight sweater that caused my heart to do a flip the way it cuddled to her superstructure.

She smiled at me as she took a large bag of groceries from the station wagon.

"Hi. So you did make it over?"

"I made it. Give me the sack." She did and our hands touched. If I hadn't been looking into her eyes, I'd never have seen the tiny flicker that went through them. I wondered what it meant. To me the touch was like brushing a live wire. Her skin had a live softly moist touch and the contact was accidental, therefore for some reason, intimate. A little wave of color came to her face as she turned to get another bag. "Load me up," I said. "Anyone as big as me should be able to take a load of groceries twice this big."

She laughed relievedly and loaded me up, bringing a few small bags herself.

We stashed the groceries and inhaled gratefully the smells coming from the kitchen.

After Laurie found out she was going to have to take me home, she asked, "How long will it take you to shower and change?"

"Oh thirty or forty minutes. I've got to shave, too, and shaving is a chore to me. I have to take it easy around all this scar tissue and whatnot."

She came close to me and I could see the compassion in her eyes. "I can't tell you how sorry I am about your face. Jack... May I call you that?"

"Of course."

"You've been hurt... Oh, I don't mean the physical pain... too many other things. Your eyes show it."

"And you've been hurt, too," I countered, matching the softness in her voice. "Maybe we can console each other."

She turned her eyes away. "It's just that I hate to see anyone brutalized."

"Oh, that was a long time ago."

"The physical part was. You've been hurt deep down. I read about the girl who was killed in your arms. It must have been a terrible thing."

"It was," I said tightly. "It's something better forgotten."

"And here I am bringing it up. I asked you how long a moment ago because every afternoon I work out on my trampoline for a few minutes. It keeps me loosened up and I enjoy it."

"Take your workout by all means. May I watch?"

For a long moment she looked at me and her face grew a little pale. "If you wish," she said at length and she went into the west wing of the clubhouse where she and her family lived.

Mrs. Stewart intercepted me as I turned to go watch Mr. Stewart work on the boat. "Jack, you'll be the only man other than her father she ever let watch her on the trampoline."

"But … why?"

"I don't know why in your case. When you see her, you'll know why in all the other cases."

Laurie came out of the house in a robe that she had wrapped primly about her from chin to ankles. She motioned to me to follow and we went into a huge green house where she had set up her equipment.

"I used to be a fair hand at this," I said as we went through the door which she closed firmly. "The coach used to make us do it to sharpen coordination and balance."

"This and dancing," she said, "are the best I know for it. Good dancing, I mean, not this hopping around stuff so many do now."

"I'll buy that. I've been called pretty square on my dancing."

We reached the edge of the trampoline and she stopped and seemed lost in thought for a moment. She turned to me and when

I looked into her eyes, I could see the emotional battle going on deep within them.

"Jack, I really shouldn't let you watch. I have never let another man watch me."

I smiled and touched her shoulders. "I'd guess because of the way you wear your robe that your trampoline costume is rather daring."

"It's more than daring. It's practically indecent."

"Then why are you letting me watch?"

She shook her head. "That's what has me puzzled. I don't really know. This is the second time I've been around you. We haven't had a total of an hour's association and here I am about to let you see me in a costume that leaves me almost naked. I want you to see me … over all my conscious objections."

I squeezed her shoulders. "I'll leave if you want me to."

Her smile was tremulous. "Then I'd have lost a battle I fought to win. Maybe I can explain everything to you some day."

"As I said yesterday, I'm easy to talk to."

"Yes, you're easy to talk to, disconcertingly so. You're easy to be around. You make this so easy when my problem is that it shouldn't be so. Why isn't it so?"

"Because you know that if you took off every stitch you have on and went through your act my only reaction would be one of outrageous appreciation."

Her lips twitched. "No desire?"

I laughed. "Desire, of course. Even with that Mother Hubbard you have on, you're desirable. I said reaction, maybe I should have said action. I'm a man, Laurie, and I don't think I missed anything that should go into a man's makeup."

She turned away and shuddered. "I know. I've watched you play ball, Jack. I've never seen such ferocity … such savagery …"

"You must have seen the game when Bob Capers slapped me silly. He made me so mad I could have killed someone."

She turned and nodded eagerly. "And the next play from scrimmage you went sixty-five yards for a touchdown. You ran over half the Ole Miss team to do it."

"Not quite," I said becoming uncomfortable. "Like I said, I'm a man and I'll stand here and enjoy watching you."

She turned and slipping out of the robe leaped lightly onto the trampoline. Now I could see what Mrs. Stewart had meant. She was clad in a white skintight thingamajig that looked something like a bathing suit but this one would never stand wetting. As it was her satiny hide shone through with a pinkish tan luminescence that made my mouth flush suddenly. It had slender shoulder straps and plunged deeply between her breasts. It must have taken considerable nerve for her not to wear a bra because the pink tips of her breasts shone like tiny bulbs through the thin white material and I could see now how taut and firm they really were. It cut her tightly in the crotch and just barely managed to encompass her rounded derriere. The dull smudge that showed through at the apex of the magic triangle I saw only when she tumbled because she kept her back to me as much as possible.

I saw the show of my life. I'd always considered myself pretty good on the thing but I saw an artist workout that afternoon. Forward and backward spins... the works. In ten minutes she was red from exertion and her hair clung to her neck and temples in sweat drenched clumps. Finally she did a really gut busting bounce and twist, came down on her feet, bounced off high in the air and sailed in my direction. I had to catch her. There was no way out of it.

She landed in my arms but her weight was nothing now. I was past such things as mere weight. I caught her, let her slide through my arms and pulling her close, I kissed her and had the rare treat of a really fabulous woman going as limp as a lapdog and she accepted my best kiss with wet twisting return. For some time our mouths were raving things, feeding and feasting then a sob she tore loose, grabbed up her robe and slipped it on while running for the door. Ten minutes later, dressed in a crisp cool cotton dress, she got in the station wagon and drove me home. Her hair was still damp and her face wore a kind of rapturous repose,

I chuckled and stretched my too long legs and relaxed.

"What's funny?" she said in a cool detached voice.

"Oh ... I almost apologized for what I did in the green house. It's almost like apologizing because I shave and wear pants. I don't think anything could have kept me from performing as I did."

She was quiet a long time and I guessed she'd rather forget it. Then she said, "Yes, I think I know how is was. I don't know why I sprang at you like I did. I don't know why I let you see me in that getup. I could have worn a bra and pants under it. I guess I'm just a terrible exhibitionist. I guess I jumped into your arms subconsciously hoping you'd do what you did."

She stopped the station wagon suddenly and bent over the wheel weeping bitterly. I didn't say anything until she began to recover. "Why do you say that, Laurie? Is it wrong for you to know that you have a beautiful body and to enjoy it?"

She made a peculiar noise and came into my arms. Just for solace and protection. She didn't want me to kiss her again. I could see that and didn't try.

"How could you know about things like that?" she said in a muffled voice.

"The girl who was killed in my arms was like that. She posed nude for me to do a figurine of her."

She sat up and dried her eyes with a tissue she pulled from purse. "I'm awful," she whispered. "Simply awful."

"What makes you say that?"

She took a deep breath and faced me. "Jack, I'll have to tell you. I couldn't be around you living a lie. You do things to me. You're too understanding and I'm water-weak when I'm around you. You know too much about people ... me. As stupid as this sounds I'm afraid I'm going to fall in love with you and you'd have to know the truth."

"All right, tell me."

"It wasn't all Hull's fault."

"I'd say no man is quite sane around you. Maybe you don't really appreciate what you have."

"I think I do. But that night we'd had a few drinks and it started simply as a lark. I teased him awfully but then when I wanted to quit, he wouldn't, and when finally it was ready to happen I lost my senses completely. I wanted it to happen, too. It did happen. I think I must have been insane. I was a demon, a beast. When I finally woke up to what was happening, I was naked and recovering from something that had never happened to me before. I can't lie about it. It was a terrible thing but it was wonderful, terribly wonderful but then I saw myself clearly and tried to fight him off. He wasn't satisfied. He wanted to make a night of it. So did I but I managed to replace passion with anger. I got one of Dad's guns and tried to brain him. I even tried to shoot him when he was out but I couldn't make the thing work because I was so overcome with remorse and rage. He got out just as Mother and Dad came in and I went into a really lurid fit of hysterics. I've hated myself ever since because I blamed him for something that was largely my own fault." She crumpled and cried hard for a few minutes while I held her close and let the purge work.

"Okay, let's go," I said lightly. "Can you drive?"

"Yes … yes, I can drive." She drove off slowly.

There was a period of silence then she said in a choking voice. "Now you can go ahead and hate me."

"Stop the buggy, Laurie."

"No … you just want to be kind. You can't really …" I smashed the brake down with my left foot and flipped the switch off. The wagon skidded a little but she compensated automatically and we stopped. I hauled her into my arms and until she was gasping for breath I kissed her as I had never kissed a woman before. I kissed her until her body was as pliant as a reed and I knew what the story was. She was like me. Women were necessary to me. Men were necessary to her. Her only protection was keeping them at arm's length. Right then I could have, right out on a public highway just before dark.

I released her and let her breathe and cry, then I gradually put her back under the wheel.

"Unless you have no woman's instinct left at all," I said softly, "you now know the answer to that 'hate me' bit. I couldn't hate you and is what you did going to be the ruination of you? You followed nature's pattern. If you have a little more nature than most, then that's what you have and all the remorse and internal battling is not going to change a thing. You see, I know, because I'm that way myself. I'm not a virgin. Could I demand that you be?"

She crumpled and cried stormily for a while then took the wheel again. "I've lost four pounds crying," she said loudly, hating herself for it. "But ... Oh, Jack, I feel so much better. Who'd believe that just after meeting you in no time at all I feel better than I have in a year?"

"You'll feel better than that before long," I told her.

CHAPTER FIFTEEN

I t was at that point that the bullet came through the windshield and I'd have run him down like a dog even if he'd have shot me to bits but a piece of flying glass bit Laurie's cheek and the blood spouted. By the time I saw that she was all right, whoever it was had gone but I found his nest and an empty .303 Enfield cartridge.

He'd been waiting there some time. The darkness had spoiled his aim. I had sense enough to pick up the empty with my handkerchief hoping it might bear fingerprints. The other one, the one that had been found in Professor Mehle's garage had some smudged prints but nothing the police could work with.

I didn't think he'd try again that night so when we got home I bathed Laurie's face and applied antiseptic and a Band-Aid.

The bullet ruined the night and I began to melt the wires to Matt Palmer who in turn alerted the State Police and although it took a while for everyone to assemble, we had a caucus that night. Laurie was cast into the background, a matter which she was too smart to resent. Matt had had the foresight to drag Benjy along and it was from Benjy we discovered most.

"I don't know what got into him," he said at the beginning of a long recital. "He started drinking and finally was of no use to us at the office at all. Gradually Charles and myself took over his duties. He drinks and stays gone for days at a time."

"How long has he been gone this time?" asked Captain Keldell of the Mississippi State Police.

"Days … I'm not sure exactly." Benjy was nervous and wanted out.

The fat red-faced sheriff, Bill Elderman, spoke up, "Like you say, Mr. McKnight, whoever fired that shot had been in the spot for some time. Several whiskey bottles were found there, paper such as food might have been wrapped in. I think in the morning I'll have my deputies comb that area."

Captain Keldell spoke up again. "That's all right as an idea, Bill, but I don't think I'd make a Roman holiday of it. He was obviously on foot and a few men scouting quietly might do a lot more good."

"It's kinda hard to keep dawgs quiet," rejoined the sheriff placidly.

"Oh … you mean bloodhounds?"

"Correct. If he's afoot, then all the better."

Even bloodhounds didn't turn up anything and in a week most people, not including me, had begun to forget it.

I went around with a .30 caliber Springfield Sporter on the back seat and one of Mr. Stewart's .45 service automatics on the front seat beside me.

Aunt Ethel fussed over me mightily and fed me until I'd gained the poundage I'd lost, but I stayed on the run as much as possible because I still hadn't seen all my acres and didn't want to get fat. This annoyed the Stewarts, it annoyed Jesse Hawkins and it simply turned Sheriff Bill Elderman purple. Matt Palmer called up and said to knock off the valor act or he'd come down and kick me naked. Helga called and said that she was expecting her second, which if it was a boy would be named after me and would I please stay alive for the event. I had Helga and Hans down for the week end once and everyone had a fine time. All but Laurie, that is.

She blew out to the place one morning and demanded an explanation.

We sat on the veranda and sipped the coffee Aunt Ethel brought for us and when the old woman had gone, Laurie faced me accusingly. "Jack, what's the matter?"

"Matter?"

"Matter! I couldn't ... I simply couldn't be wrong about how you felt that afternoon. Now you never come to the Lodge. I never see you."

I'd known this had to happen. "Laurie, until this mad dog is found, I certainly don't want you to get hurt. Have you forgotten what happened to Freida Mehle? Do you think I can forget it?"

She caught her breath. "I hadn't forgotten," she said in a low voice. "I'd pushed myself ahead of the memory. I'm very sorry, Jack."

"Your reference to that evening was quite correct. It happened awfully fast but things just seem to happen that way around me. I've known two girls of whom I thought a great deal. They're both dead. I can't see that happen to you."

"I know ... I know ..." Her eyes came up and met mine. "Did you love them, Jack?" She shook her head. "Don't answer that. I had no right to ask it."

"I don't mind answering it. What I felt for Ginger wasn't what I felt for Freida. What I felt for Freida is not what I feel for you. There are points of similarity but there is no conflict if that's what you want to know."

She smiled but it trembled a little. "I think that was what I wanted to hear more than anything else."

Winter hardened the world and I got sucked into the muscle end of raising cattle because we were shorthanded and we had some problems that needed a strong back, not genius. I qualified for the former I saw Laurie occasionally but there was little closeness to the meetings, usually in company of others. I didn't like it that way and neither did she, but that's the way it had to be. Time went on its way as it does habitually and also habitually it caused minds to dull and memories to dim. Laurie wasn't a girl I could stay away from, especially knowing that not only was she about the loveliest thing on two feet but unless something happened she was mine for the taking. That state had existed for a long time and there was a little voice nagging me along the line that if I didn't take her soon, impatience was going to cause trouble.

More than that I wanted to make a figure of her, nude of course, and I had asked her to let her hair grow although I hadn't told her why. It improved her looks. It was now just at the nape of her neck, reaching for shoulder length, not quite making it. It moved softly when she'd toss her head and when she'd work out on her trampoline it would swish and flare and become disordered. I'd taken to joining her and I'll never forget my first time. After that big first of hers, she'd worn another costume which while no thicker than the white one was of dark blue and revealed nothing but outline. Naturally, there was plenty of that to reveal. I'd used tight lastex swimming trunks and wasn't ashamed of the figure I made in them because though I'd gained weight. I was still in good condition. I did my best which certainly didn't come up to her worst, but she watched me with a rapt expression on her face and finally when I was winded, I did a forward bounce and somersault and landed in the peat moss at her feet.

Her fingertips touched my arms, flanks and hips. "You've such a beautiful body," she said softly.

I'm sure I blushed. I'd been called a lot of things but never beautiful.

"It's hard and sinewy and so big. You've such perfect control of it …" Then very gently she came into my arms and rested quietly against me. She didn't raise her face for a kiss and I didn't try to push her into it.

I held her for a long time and the taste of her exciting body came through my skin like a heated fog. I could feel the steady strong beat of her heart and the points of her breasts were like an electric contact.

She looked up and her eyes were wet, the lashes long and shiny and dank with tears. "Why are we so close? More so than a lot of married people. Where on earth did I get the nerve to let you see me in that white thing?" She shuddered and clung to me as though for protection.

"Maybe fate got tired of us playing around, Laurie. Maybe she stepped in and gave us a shove.

"Maybe. Will you accept the shove?"

"Yes."

Her eyes widened and her breath came faster. "Then …" She stopped hard. She couldn't say it so I said it for her. "I want to marry you. If I loved you more it would be abnormal."

"Oh … Jack …" She clung to me and went into a fit of shuddering and crying.

"When?" I asked after she'd regained control.

"Now … tomorrow, the week end, next week. What does it matter? I'm not going any place." The relief was such that I went as weak as a cat and she was weaker. We sort of crumpled to the sawdust floor and somehow we kissed and two people who'd been beaten around by life considerably almost went to pieces in the wonder of our love.

"Please, Jack." She was resisting me with such gentleness that it was almost like acceptance. "Not here … please."

"Right," I said thickly getting to my feet. I brushed the sawdust from her satiny hide then she performed a like office for me.

"Wedding or no wedding, we take an early swim … in your creek," she said with such deadly intent that I was momentarily startled.

I nodded. "What sort of wedding shall it be?"

"Small and quiet. Okay?"

"To the tenth power. Small but how quiet my friends will let it be I can't promise. If it's all right with you I want Matt, Jerry and Mamma Palmer, Helga and Hans Van Peit, Professor Mehle and Stan Modeleski. I'll never be able to repay these people for what they've done for me and I want them to see the most important thing that will ever happen to me."

She smiled and it was something holy about it. "Of course, you shall have anyone you want."

"And you?"

"Just Mother and Dad...and you, of course." We laughed a great deal over her words although there was nothing very funny about them. We needed to laugh. We were in a laughing mood now. It was a great feeling.

Our swimming day was destined to be another one of those days when too much happened. Things that happened to me always seemed to burst out all at once in a single twenty-four hours.

I dropped by on my horse to pick Laurie up and Stonewall Stewart and Eadie his wife came to meet me as I hitched my mount.

"Shy sort, ain't you?" said Stoney grinning widely.

"Be quiet," said Eadie looking almost as young as her daughter. "You've got the boy blushing."

Stoney took my hand and wrung it hard. "We're glad, boy...plenty glad."

Eadie tiptoed and kissed me. "Indeed we are glad, son. I think you're the one for her. I felt it even before I saw you so maybe you can forgive me for kind of pushing it along."

"I wanted it that way," I said seriously. "You just made it easy for me."

"I think she took her tumble about thirty minutes after she met you," said Stoney and looking over his shoulder he said, "Uh oh. Here she comes."

"I said he wasn't to be heckled," said Laurie walking toward us with the consummate grace that was her birthright.

"Not guilty," said Stoney. "As parents we felt we had to say something."

I laughed. "They aren't heckling me, Laurie. After all, they're headed for in-law parenthood so they have some right."

She smiled and kissed me lightly. "I was kidding of course. Ready?"

"All ready."

"Where," asked Stoney, "is your gun?"

I started. I'd been in such a rosy haze I'd completely forgotten about Jake, guns and anything else that wasn't a happy thought. "I forgot it," I said shamefacedly.

"I didn't," said Laurie producing a snub nosed .38 revolver from her back jeans pocket.

"That ought to do it," I said feeling a chill in my belly.

"Not on your life," said Stoney positively. "You people who feel smug just because you have one little popgun annoy me. Wait here."

He went into the house and from his collection brought me a small cannon. It was a .44 Magnum and weighed something over four pounds. "Gad, what a field piece," I said hefting the mighty weapon.

"You have my forty-five," he said. "I have some twenty-twos and a thirty-two but they're pop guns. Let someone have one of these slugs in the gut you'll blow him in half."

I tucked the gun in my belt and felt pretty silly and he saw it. "Sure you feel silly but you'd feel a hell of a lot sillier if that bird who's after you got the drop on you and you didn't have anything."

We left with Rex trying to catch Laurie's mare's attention without much success so he sulked all the way to the creek. The heavy gun annoyed me so I dropped it into a saddle bag.

Following Laurie at a leisurely pace a cataract of thoughts poured through my mind. My mother ... I'd ducked the matter in my mind. I'd ducked pressing Eadie about her. There were reasons for this. Like Eadie said, it wasn't her secret alone. There were others involved. I was slightly involved myself. Someday I'd know. I was sure of it. I watched the slender witchery of Laurie's body as she swayed in perfect rhythm to her mare's gait, the willow switch flexibility of her every move, the exciting action of her classic bottom on the shallow saddle. I felt I knew what we were riding to and it wasn't a swim. Maybe an incidental dip but it was something else that had made Laurie insist with peculiar fierceness on the swim...today and let nothing interfere with it. Wedding plans could wait. This had to happen. Now she was riding straight for it...whatever it was, her fine head up and her eyes straight ahead. I felt a strange sort of thrill tickle my spine.

I was so drowned in my own deep study that Rex stopped by himself as Laurie slipped from her mare and tied her in a dense thicket of youpon and pine.

A flush was on her cheek and her eyes sparkled like gems. "Come on, I'll show you my hideout."

"You've been here before, I take it?"

She made a face at me. "The last time I was here you spied on me." With a leap she came into my arms and cuddled there for protection as was her habit at times. She didn't especially want to be loved or kissed or fondled. She just wanted to be reassured by my presence and that fact that in my arms she was safe and cozy.

"Jack," it was almost a whisper, "you're so good for me. So good to me."

I felt like a heel. If I was good to and for her, what was she to me? All of a sudden I felt humble and unworthy. I left like performing some act of humility before her and the only thing I could think of I did. I slipped to the ground on my knees and embraced her around the waist and hips, pressing my face into the slightly rounded platter of her stomach that was trembling with emotion. She slid through my arms and to her knees. She caught my face in her hands and stared at me. I couldn't see her through the dimness of my eyes except as a watery wraith of heart wrenching loveliness.

"Why did you do that?" she asked slowly placing her face against mine and holding me gently close.

"Because it was the only thing I could think of to do. You broke my back with that talk about what I'd done for you. Maybe I'm not as vocal as you but there's one thing sure. You've done things for me, too. You picked me out of a sea of sickness and fear and dread. You made me want to live and love again."

She stood up and pulled at my hands and when I was standing with her she kissed me. Her fabulous lips as smooth as butter and so meltingly soft that I felt giddy.

"So," she said in her warm caressing voice, "we both feel that way and we're going to be married. Could you improve on that?"

"I don't think so. It's just that every time I look at you under the most normal of circumstances I'm overloaded. Think of an overload on top of an overload."

"It's easy," she said lightly. "It's happened to me so many times since you came to live among us. Now away to the hideout before the bandits catch us."

The hideaway was something any fifteen year old kid would have given his all to possess. In flood times the creek had broadened at the rapids and the backwash had hollowed out of the sandstone a globular cave some six feet wide and three high at the entrance but on the inside the ceiling was a good eight feet high. The floor was sandy and at the far end where the cave narrowed to a corridor maybe two feet in diameter was a big pile of something. When my eyes became accustomed to the dim light I could see that the pile was a huge party blanket that had been pegged down at all four corners and underneath was a thick strata of Spanish moss. Her breath came fast and as she hugged my left arm I could feel the tremors flitting through her body. One firm breast dug into my biceps.

"Do you like it?"

"Wonderful," I said rather breathlessly because now I knew for sure something I'd thought but hadn't been certain about.

"Oh, it took a lot of work," she said stepping to one side and pointing. "I had to level the sand and throw out an awful lot of junk... driftwood and the like that the eddies threw into the place."

"When did you do it?" I asked.

She faced me. "Since the last big rain." She let it rest at that but I caught it. It hadn't been done long.

"I was afraid another rain would come and ruin it all."

I tried to take her in my arms but she backed away, her eyes wide and her breath coming fast.

"Please, Jack... please don't touch me."

I waited. She seemed actually afraid now but I knew it couldn't be so.

A sob caught in her throat. "Let's just lie down here side by side." She choked back another sob and caught me by the hand. We stretched out on the comfortable if crude bed. I took my place a generous two feet from her but she rolled over and came close. "I'll have to talk to you... I'm not rejecting you but you see I don't want to flip like... I mean I don't want to turn into a raging beast. I can, you know." She levered herself up on her elbows, her eyes swimming with tears and lines of pain cutting her face. "With Hull I found out what I could be like. I'm telling you this so you'll understand. I made my mistake when I foolishly tried to tease him. I didn't realize that I was teasing myself, too. I didn't expect him to overpower me. He did, then I didn't need overpowering. I went insane. I hardly even remember it in detail. All I can remember is that if I'd died the next minute, I had to have him. That was what has had me so bitter... toward myself, not what happened. So... please, Jack, let's just lie here a while very quietly." She levered herself closer. "You do believe I love you?"

I didn't move. I just looked at her. "Of course I do. You wouldn't be here if you didn't."

She sank back and breath stuttered into her throat. "Thanks for saying it like that. What a wonderful compliment."

We lay quiet for a long time, her shoulder touching mine, the curve of her hip warming my side. Finally her hand touched mine and closed on it convulsively.

"Jack, would you hate me terribly if I turn out to be a thorough bitch?"

I laughed. "I think that any woman who qualifies for the term lady then tries to maintain that same attitude in more profound performances is a dead bust. I hope to hell you're the most unfettered bitch I ever encountered in my life."

She sat up and let loose a few bars of silvery laughter. It startled me. She thrust her hands through her silky soft hair and let it fall in disorder.

"Oh God, what a wonderful feeling to be free, to feel that even if I am a bitch my man will love it … just because it's me." She turned and fell across me, her lips close to mine. She caught my face and held it tightly. "Thanks for saying that. Thanks for saying it so I know you mean it." She kissed me but before it could generate any heat she withdrew. She sat away from me and said, "Turn your back" Her eyes were feverishly bright and her breathing was as though she'd been in a foot race.

I turned my back. "Do I have to do this? I'd like to watch."

She caught me by the shoulder and pulled me to her. She wore only her jeans now. "I'm being silly," she said throatily. "Of course you can watch. You can even help."

I caught her close and threw my everything into a kiss that backfired and almost blinded me. Her back was so miraculously soft and fine and the pressure of her breasts with their red erect tips were a sweet agony where they touched me.

She tore away again. "Please don't let me lose my grip." She backed away, unashamed of the magnificent leap of the twin towers of feminity. "Pull," she said, happiness and a curious exultance coloring her voice. She offered me her feet and I caught the jeans and tugged them from her. All she wore now was a foggy gesture of nylon about her middle. She leaped and caught me, her mouth finding mine momentarily and rejecting it immediately. "Just hold me and let me catch on again." I held her shuddering body, my own beginning a savage response that was shoving me dangerously close to the breaking point.

I tried to kiss her but she avoided me and begged me to let her get quiet again.

She was fairly quiet now and I thought I knew what to do. She, oddly, wished to avoid the wild frenzied excitement that sometimes turns a woman into a cannibalistic savage … if she could. She had worked hard at it and I couldn't help admire the rocky fortitude she'd exhibited. Suddenly I drew her close and gripped her with such strength that a thready little whine of pain or expectation trickled from her throat.

And she'd been right. The frenzy never appeared except in certain moments when we were the center of a white hot world of puffy nothingness. Things were different now. I was hers for all time and some of the fearful pressures were now absent. She wept from an overloaded heart, a joy her senses could not accept without some obeisance from her. She wept from utter fatigue and she wept from the clean peaceful release that went through her veins like a drug.

We were close in a tangle that grew from the necessity of being closer than it was possible for two people to be and, of course, it was at this point when we were drugged and sated, not of this world but of another lighter, brighter, cleaner place, it happened.

The bush that almost obscured the opening of the cave was torn bodily away and the flood of light was almost as shocking as Jake's voice.

"All right, Kingpin … unwind."

His face was puffed and red and brutal and in his hands was the short stubby Enfield we had wondered about. He squatted so he could see all and a grating chuckle burst from his thick throat.

"How very convenient. If you recall, Kingpin, I promised you this. I promised you that you'd suffer and beg and lick my feet. You'll do all that and it won't do any good. While I have my fun with the little lady, my friend will hold the gun on you. Then it will be his turn … then mine … then his. After that, you'll get to watch us in operation. First on her because I want you to see it all to the very last breath she draws. Then we'll take our good time on you. Nice picture, hunh, boy who always gets the lush women?" It poured out of him, a cauldron of hate. "Nice soft women. Nothing but the best for my brother. I got one of them and almost got you. I was wrong. I might have gotten you both but that would have been a mistake." Saliva was drooling from his mouth now and I was shaking like in a hard chill. "Well, we'll get along with it." He straightened up and began to talk to someone else nearby.

"Where's your gun?" I asked in a sharp hiss.

She choked on the answer. "Way over there all messed up in my clothes." With a flip such as no one but a trampoline expert could have made, she bounced away, darted to her clothes, made a frenzied two-second search, failed to find it, then simply disappeared ... vanished. There was the little two foot corridor but it dead ended a few feet further on I knew but she'd gone like a doused light.

Jake's face framed the entrance again the rifle pointing at me. "Where'd she go?" he snarled savagely.

I shrugged. "How would I know? You can see there's no place for her to go."

He couldn't see the corridor and for a moment I thought he'd dropped his marbles for sure. For some time he raved and ranted, his eyes red and gleaming like a mad dog's and I knew that nothing short of a miracle could save us. They'd drag me out and search the cave. They'd find her jammed up at the dead end of the little tunnel and that would be all she wrote. It was then that I made up my mind that I couldn't be any deader trying to live and if I saw the remotest flicker of a chance, I was going to make the most of it.

"Come on over here, you damn yellow bellied bastard," roared Jake and it was then that I saw who his partner was. Tom Hull. Tom was white faced and wanted out but he was too deep in now. "Get in there and find that bitch," snarled Jake shoving Tom through the entrance. I thought of grabbing Tom and using him as a shield but I knew that wouldn't stop Jake for a second. That .303 would dance right on through Tom and through me, too.

Tom found the corridor and if he'd been scalded he couldn't have gotten out faster. He was panting and his face was drenched with sweat. He pointed a trembling hand. "She got out," he screamed "That tunnel, it goes out the back." He had his pistol in his hand. He knew what Laurie could do with a hand gun.

The news stunned Jake for a moment then he began to curse and rave again. Tom was for more direct action and his future didn't look too bright right then. He'd been saved from Stonewall Stewart once but if she got back with the news this time, the whole world wouldn't be big enough to save him.

A ringing voice stopped Tom just as he moved from the cave mouth and then I could see it all. She stood on a slab of sandstone some twenty feet away and in her hands was Stoney's big Magnum.

"Drop it, Tom," she said crisply but he didn't. He jerked and fired at her point blank…and missed. Then my ears seemed to come apart from the terrific muzzle blast of the weapon. She was holding it with both hands, holding it tight, and down low but even then the recoil rocked her back a step. Tom Hull was flung backwards as though he'd been struck with a sledge, back into the pool where he landed with a splash, his gun flying out of his hands like a bird. She turned her attention to Jake who, like me, was frozen momentarily and was she a picture, as slim as a naiad, as nude as a boiled egg, her magnificent breasts standing forth like sensitive antenna, her blue eyes crackling with latent ferocity, her fine legs spread wide and now both thumbs caught the bat ear of the hammer and snucked it back.

"Drop it, fat boy," she said in a clear cold voice. It was then that I made my move and it almost was the end of me because at that moment Jake swung up the rifle muzzle and fired. Laurie staggered back a couple of steps and when the muzzle of the Magnum came up again I thought I could see the grey nose of the bullet in the cylinder and I did a fast roll and the bullet smashed a huge hunk of sandstone from the cave mouth missing me by inches. Jake worked the bolt of his rifle with hysterical speed and fired at Laurie again who was on her knees now trying to bring up the muzzle of the gun again.

I screamed at her with all my might not to fire and springing to my feet I swung my right arm back and never in all my career did I ever equal the effort I expended at that moment. With all the power, with every ounce of my two hundred and fifteen pounds, I smashed, Jake with the edge of my hand exactly at the junction of his neck and shoulder. My hand seemed to blow up in a balloon of flaming agony but I'd had the exquisite feeling of hearing the sickening snap of his neck and so what if I'd broken a hand doing it? Then swallowing nausea from the pain, I dashed to Laurie who was trying to stagger to her feet. A bullet had entered just below her right breast and travelling just under the skin come out without, if I was any judge, doing a lot of damage. It hadn't felt like a caress and she was a little groggy from shock. I tore up a T shirt and bound it roughly, slipped her shirt on over it and pulled it close and tied the tail. Then I brought her panties and felt like a husband helping her into them. Then came her jeans and shoes and socks. She smiled at me wanly as she sat on the old water washed log and watched me clumsily lace up her saddle oxfords.

"Did I do all right, Jack?"

I had to laugh. Had she done all right? "If you don't get the Congressional Medal, I'm going to set fire to the Pentagon. You not only got Hull, you gave me a chance to get Jake."

"We'd better tie him up."

"If I'm that wrong, I'm going to take up embroidery for a living. If Jake ever moves again, it'll be when they come get him in a basket."

I got up and still shuddering from the leaping arcs of pain that jumped from my hand with every heartbeat, I walked over to Jake and looked down. He was flat on his stomach and both shoulders were pressed into the sand but Jake was looking at me.

"Don't worry about Jake." I walked to the pool and got to the edge just as the boiling current cast Hull up to the top for a moment. The bullet had entered just above his navel, gone on through and smashed an exit in his back that was as big as a grapefruit. I turned away and gritted my teeth from nausea. Hull and my hand. It had nothing to do with Jake. I looked at him again and felt a sort of sadistic pride as I did. I'd never followed Jake and tried to kill him. He followed me and now it was he who lay dead at my feet. It wouldn't bring Frieda back...

"Think you can ride now?" I asked her.

"If you'll help me up. Once on, I can stick." And she did.

EPILOGUE

The hand was broken all right. Two bones but though it pained to beat everything, it was the only pain I ever actually enjoyed.

The wedding went off as scheduled and though I couldn't shake hands with anyone and played the invalid as hard as I could, it didn't keep Modeleski and Matt Palmer from beating my shoulder blades black and blue.

"How'n hell did Hull ever get to know Jake?" I asked Matt in a lull of festivity.

Matt shook his head. "We'll never know, but we know that for as long as Hull was on the place he and Jake had been systematically looting it. Mostly it was rustling of the grade stuff because that was harder to stop or trace. Only lately had they tried to raid the registered stuff and that got Hawkins to bird doggin'."

It was a glorious day and in the midst of merriment, suddenly something struck me. The big fine looking severely brunette middle aged woman who kept watching me. For some reason, no one had introduced us but what with all the feasting and revelry, that wasn't odd.

I cornered Laurie's mother. "Mrs. Stewart …" I felt choky and frightened. "May I ask you a question?"

"Of course," she said warmly.

"Is … I mean … is that her?"

She caught my forearms and her eyes were as soft as pansies. "Yes, son. That's her. Do you want to speak to her?"

The choking was worse. I nodded.

"Shall I introduce you?"

"No ... I think I'd like to speak to her alone."

I did and I've never been sorry.

THE END

www.ingramcontent.com/pod-product-compliance
Lightning Source LLC
Chambersburg PA
CBHW052009240626

47153CB00008B/2800